★ American Girl®

GIRL OF THE YEAR 2017 ★

GABRIELA

by Teresa E. Harris

Scholastic Inc.

Published by Scholastic Inc., *Publishers since 1920*. SCHOLASTIC and associated logos are trademarks and/or registered trademarks of Scholastic Inc. The publisher does not have any control over and does not assume any responsibility for author or third-party websites or their content.

This book is a work of fiction. Names, characters, places, and incidents are either the product of the author's imagination or are used fictitiously, and any resemblance to actual persons, living or dead, business establishments, events, or locales is entirely coincidental and not intended by American Girl or Scholastic Inc.

Cover photos ©: Getty Images: window (Nisian Hughes), floor (RapidEye); Shutterstock, Inc./FreshPaint: brick wall

Book design by Angela Jun

americangirl.com/service

ISBN 978-1-338-13698-2

10 9 8 7 6 5 4 3 2 1   17 18 19 20 21

Printed in the U.S.A 58 • First printing 2017

This one is for Linda.

— T.H.

Contents

Like a Roller Coaster

Chapter 1

Toe-heel-toe-heel-toe-heel-STOMP.
Toe-heel-toe-heel-toe-heel-STOMP.

Each move burst into my head like a shout. All around me the air was filled with the sounds of tap shoes scraping and stomping, Mama calling out the next step as she snapped in time to the rhythm of the music. Above me, the sun poured through Liberty's stained-glass windows, leaving little pools of colored light on the floor at my feet.

Riff-heel-ball change-riff-heel-stomp.
Riff-heel-ball change-riff-heal-tuuuuuuurrn.

I stood on my right leg and whirled around, careful to find my spot so I wouldn't get dizzy. My spot was always the same in dance studio number seven: The hollowed-out square cut into the wall right between the two big mirrors.

Gabriela

A phone niche, Mama called it, from the time when phones were so big people had to literally carve out space for them.

Toe-heel-toe-heel-toe-heel-chug.

Toe-heel-scuff-heel-tip-heel-SLAM!

My feet flew over the dance studio's worn wooden floor, from one puddle of light to another, and soon my heart was pounding out a rhythm in time with the beat, like the music and I had become one. I couldn't help it. I closed my eyes. I knew what Mama would say if she caught me: "Gabriela McBride, you know how unsafe that is? And you can lose your place that way!"

I did know that, but I knew Liberty better. Knew every spot on its dance floors, scuffed white from years of dancers like me stomping, turning, and tapping. And I knew that when I opened my eyes, a few beats from now, I'd see Liberty's painted-over brick walls, exposed heating pipes, and its tin-tiled ceiling. And I'd have no trouble finding my place.

"And . . . finish," Mama said as she turned the volume down on the old sound system we used during tap rehearsal. The music faded and then disappeared. I opened my eyes just as Mama began to clap.

"If I didn't know any better," said Mama, "I would think I was in the presence of Savion Glover's dancers."

Like a Roller Coaster

Mama beamed at each member of the Liberty Junior Dance Company in turn. When her eyes met mine, she winked. I winked back.

Mama, or Miss Tina as all the other students called her, was the founder and executive director of Liberty, also known as Liberty Arts Center, a community center she'd started seventeen years ago. Not only was Mama the "Big Kahuna" (that's what Daddy called her), she was also the director of dance programs, which suited her just fine. Mama, with her strong, powerful legs and fluid movements, always said dancing came naturally to her, like breathing. And then she'd say, "It's like that for you, too, Gabby."

It was true. Dancing came to me as easily as coding came to my best friend, Teagan, or the way words came to my cousin, Red. Or the way words seemed to come to almost everyone else, except me.

I glanced up at the clock as Mama instructed us to take a seat on the floor. My heart was still racing, and as the clock crept closer to six, my pulse sped up. I had somewhere important to be.

"Excellent work today, ladies! You're almost ready for our Rhythm and Views show next month."

Five fifty-five. I stared at Mama, willing her eyes to meet mine. When at last she looked over at me, I looked at the clock and back at her. She nodded. She hadn't forgotten she'd given me permission to skip ballet rehearsal and go to the poetry group meeting instead. I half listened as Mama rattled off dates, expectations, and information about costumes.

"Remember how much Rhythm and Views means to Liberty and to the wider community," Mama said. "Sixteen years this show has gone on, and people always come up to me and say—"

I finished Mama's sentence in my head: *that they look forward to this day all year.* The Liberty community loved the show because we got to celebrate all the hard work we'd done in the last year. Art students got to exhibit their work in the lobby and guests could even purchase the artwork, just like at a real art gallery. The dance companies performed the pieces we'd been perfecting all year. An empanada take-out joint from across the street catered the snack bar, and everyone's friends and family came out for the show. It was like a block party, cookout, and concert all rolled into one, and it was my favorite day, too.

Mama finished her speech and then clapped loudly again, her way of signaling that it was time to go.

I jumped to my feet, ran over to where I'd left my bag, and tore off my tap shoes. In four seconds flat, I was bolting toward the door in my sneakers, pausing just long enough to wave to Mama. She smiled and shook her head. I guess she was as surprised as I still sometimes was that I was in a hurry to get to a place where I'd have to stand up and talk in front of other people.

See, talking wasn't like dancing for me. When I danced tap or hip-hop, I could speak with my feet. My hands. My whole body, if I wanted to. I could make one move quiet as a whisper, the next loud as a shout. But sometimes, when I opened my mouth, it was like my words started to second-guess themselves. Like they weren't sure if they wanted to come out and when they finally did, I started stuttering like crazy.

But not all the time.

Like when I was racing to the dance studio where the poetry group met, I ran straight into Amelia Sanchez, my ballet instructor. "Whoa, Gabby, slow down," she said, laughing. "I spoke to your mom. You're going to make up tonight's missed rehearsal, right?"

"I definitely am," I said, without a single stutter.

I kept on going. And when I ran into good old Stan, the friendliest janitor ever, he said, "Where are you hurrying off to, Gabby?" and I replied, "Poetry club meeting. See you later!" without missing a beat.

Gabriela

Mrs. Baxter, my speech therapist at school, told me that people who stutter don't do it as much in places they feel comfortable. That's why my speech was hardly ever bumpy when I was in our little white-and-blue house on Tompkins Street with Mama and Daddy or at Liberty, because both places were home to me, both places filled with family. Like Amelia, who I'd known since she was nineteen and I was six. She taught me how to spot on my turns by challenging me to a staring contest. "Every time you turn, I want us eye-to-eye." Even now, four years later, if Amelia thought I wasn't spotting she'd gently say, "Staring contest, Gabby," to remind me. Stan was like family, too. I'd known him my whole life—he'd been the janitor at Liberty ever since Mama opened it.

"Hold on there now," Stan called out, and I stopped in my tracks. "Poetry's been moved to the auditorium, hasn't it?"

Shoot! How had I forgotten? I took off in the other direction, calling, "Thanks, Stan," over my shoulder as I went.

By the time I made it to the auditorium, the whole group was already up onstage. For the second time, I stopped in my tracks. I'd danced on that very same stage plenty of times, but today was the very first time I'd have to *speak* on it. I gulped.

Like a Roller Coaster

"Gabby, over here!"

Teagan called to me with a frantic wave of her hand. The poetry group had made a circle onstage in front of the heavy red curtain, and Teagan had saved me a seat right beside her.

"I've got everything ready to go," she whispered to me, reaching up to adjust her beanie over her strawberry-blonde hair. There were two things Teagan was almost never without: her coding notebook (she'd named it Cody) and her turquoise beanie.

"Got what ready to go?" I asked.

"The you-know-what that we've been working on?" Teagan wriggled her eyebrows. "You *know*, the *surprise*?"

"Oh, right!" I wiped my sweaty hands on my leggings.

"Are you okay, Gabby?"

"Y-Yes," I stammered. But Teagan knew me better than almost anyone.

"You're nervous about saying your poem in front of Bria and Alejandro, right?" Teagan sat up on her knees and faced me. She was in full-on Teagan Problem-Solving Mode. "Just relax and remember to think about each word before you say it. Give it time to form in your mind. Don't rush. Okay?"

I nodded again. "Okay."

Gabriela

Just then, my cousin Red emerged from behind the curtain, rubbing his hands together and smiling big enough to show off the right front tooth he'd chipped last summer when he hit a curb and flew over the handlebars of his bike. "All right, poets," he said. "Tonight we say bye-bye to that old dance studio and hello to the stage. We're big-time now, ready for crowds skyscraper-high touching clouds."

Red had been staying with my family for the past four months, ever since his mom, Mama's sister and a military doctor, had gotten called back to active duty. At first, I didn't like Red being around too much—for the first few weeks after he arrived, I called him the Interloper until Mama and Daddy told me to stop. But it wasn't my fault Red was *always* in the upstairs bathroom *exactly* when I needed to use it. Plus, he was loud, like two-trains-crashing-into-each-other loud, and he never missed a chance to remind me that he was going into seventh grade and I was only going into sixth.

But, I had to admit Red had a way with words. He could spin a line of poetry like I could pas de bourrée. He lived and breathed poetry, and wanted to bring it to Liberty in the form of a club—nothing too formal. Mama was 100 percent behind the idea and, because I was supposed to be showing Red he was welcome and *not* an interloper, Mama said,

Like a Roller Coaster

"Gabby, you should join, too." She'd made it sound like a suggestion, but it was really an order.

I hadn't wanted to join at first—spoken words are your enemy when you stutter—but words just seemed to flow whenever the poetry group got together. Even mine—most of the time.

"So, the Rhythm and Views show is our first chance to show everyone what we've got," Red was saying.

I imagined Teagan's grandfather, who was the visual arts instructor and the unofficial program director, preparing his art students, too. Everyone—dancers, artists, and this year, poets, too—was a part of Rhythm and Views, and everyone needed to be ready.

"And we need to show them that we've got mad talent," Red was saying. "Which is why everything's got to be perfect. Our poems, the order, everything. Alejandro, can you handle the spotlight for me?"

"On it," Alejandro replied. He was tall and pencil-skinny with thick black hair that came to the middle of his back. Red sometimes liked to joke that Alejandro's hair weighed more than he did. As Alejandro rose and climbed up to the lighting booth, Red pulled a list from the front pocket of his shorts. On it was a list of names. The order of performances. I was first.

First!

"Ready, Gabby?" Red asked. "You can do it. You're big-time now."

"Ready for crowds," a girl named Bria chimed in.

"Skyscraper-high," shouted Alejandro, coming out from the booth at the back of the theater.

"T-Touching clouds," I finished quietly.

"Yes!" Red cried, clapping loudly. Soon everyone else joined in.

As I got to my feet, the applause died down.

"Take center stage, Gabby," Red said, pointing.

I moved to the middle of the circle and looked out at the sea of chairs. The spotlight shined directly on me. *Big-time now, ready for crowds.*

"Ssssssspeaking ough-ought to be—" I began, and then I stopped. My face grew hot. I hated stuttering in front of my friends. Maybe I could tell Red to come back to me at the end.

"You were doing great, Gabby," Alejandro called out.

"Keep going," said Red.

"Slow down and think about each word," Teagan put in.

Mama and Daddy were always telling me that while it was good to work with Mrs. Baxter, I shouldn't let my bumpy speech stop me from talking. "We love you no matter how many sounds you make," they'd say. "Say what you have to say! We're always listening."

"Okay." Another deep breath. Then I started over.

"Speaking ought to be, ought to be like . . . like
   breathing
Words always there, no need for . . . reaching
Like cracking a jjjjjjoke is for a joker
But for me it's like a roller coaster . . . coaster"

I paused. I knew this poem and even bigger than that, I knew these people. Red. Teagan. Alejandro. Bria. I knew this space, too, Liberty's auditorium. I knew there were 480 seats, but only 476 worked. I knew seat 3L was the best in the house, that one of the angels carved into the balcony was cross-eyed, and that there was a corner where every word you said echoed throughout the auditorium, even if you whispered. *You're home, Gabby*, I told myself, and picked up my poem where I left off.

"Up, up, up and then racing . . . racing to the
   g-ground

Gabriela

Words flying by me that I can't pin down

Words soar past me, whip my face like . . . like air
In my mind, in my heart, everywhere
I . . . I ch-chase those wwwwords down
But when I try to speak, I don't make a sound

Up, up, up and then racing to the ground
Words flying by me that I can't pin down

Sometimes my words get caught
Come grinding to a halt
I slip, I fall, I stutter
But it's not my fault

Up, up, up and then racing to the ground
Words flying by me that I can't pin down."

The applause was instantaneous. So was my smile. I'd
made it through my whole poem, and by the end I wasn't
stuttering at all! I took a deep, exaggerated bow. And then
another, and then curtsied until the rest of the poetry group
was either laughing or calling out, "Brava, brava!" or
"Encore, encore!"

Like a Roller Coaster

Red, still beaming, held up his hand for silence. "No time for encores, but awesome job, Gabby." He walked over and gave me a high five. "Bria, you're up."

Bria, a tall, round-faced girl with a big, bushy ponytail, took center stage as I slid back into my place next to Teagan. Bria, like Alejandro and Red, was going into seventh grade and when Red had told her about the poetry group, she'd joined immediately.

"Nice job," Teagan mouthed. Then she reached into the pocket of her jeans and pulled out a flash drive. "Ready for later?" she whispered.

I nodded. I felt ready for anything.

The rest of the performances flew by, and I still couldn't believe how far we'd all come since Red had first started the poetry club. And even more than that, I couldn't wait for the show. Poetry, dancing, and—

"Gabby and I have a surprise," Teagan announced, just as Alejandro, the final poet, took his seat. "We've been working on something for the show, a little something visual to go with our poetry. Wait right here."

Teagan jumped to her feet, pulling me with her. We darted around the curtain and backstage, where there was a laptop sitting on top of a podium. Wires snaked down the side of the podium like vines. To anyone else all of those wires would have been intimidating. But not to Teagan. In one smooth motion, she plugged the projector adapter into the laptop, inserted her flash drive, and said, "Can you get the main power switch for the podium and projector?" She pointed at a black box hanging on the wall behind us. It looked like a very large, very expensive version of the circuit breaker in our garage, only, I realized after pulling the box open, much more complicated. Inside were three rows of buttons and switches, all glowing a faint shade of neon green.

"Um, Teagan?"

"On it," Teagan replied, and hurried over. She pointed at a big silver button on top of all the others. "This one turns on the main power for all the stage equipment. It's kind of cool how it all works. You see, this main box controls—"

"Teagan," I cut in. Sometimes, when Teagan started talking tech, she couldn't stop.

"Sorry!" Teagan said, laughing. "Ready?"

I nodded. We reached for the button, both of our fingers pushing it at the same time.

And everything went black.

So Long for Now

Chapter 2

"W hat just happened?" I whispered to Teagan.

"I . . . I don't know."

I couldn't see her face, but I could tell from the quake in Teagan's voice that she was as panicked as I was. From the other side of the curtain came the sound of uncertain foot-shuffling and frantic whispers.

"What's going on?"

"Use the flashlight app on your phone!"

"Oh no!"

"Sorry! Was that your foot?"

"No. It was my phone!"

In the darkness, Teagan groped for my hand. Together we felt our way to the curtain and back to the stage, where cell phone flashlights were bobbing about, lighting up confused faces. Except for Bria, who alternated between staring down at the cracked screen of her phone and glaring at Alejandro.

"What happened?" asked Red, shining the light of his phone on Teagan and me.

I didn't know, but I remembered what Mama always told me to do in case of an emergency in the center.

"Parking lot," I said.

Using the phone flashlights as a guide, we filed down the stage stairs and out of the side door of the auditorium. The parking lot was already full of dancers and some of the people from Mr. Harmon's art class. They were milling around, looking just as confused as the rest of us. I spotted Mama immediately. She still wore her tap shoes—a big no-no outside—and her face was a mask of worry. I ran over to her, pulling Teagan along with me.

"Mama, w-what's going on?" I asked, but just then Mr. Harmon, Teagan's grandfather, came out of the building with the rest of his art class trailing behind him. He went right over to Mama.

"Could be a thrown fuse in the circuit box," he said, raking his hand through his salt-and-pepper hair. "Let me grab the flashlight from my trunk."

And just like that, Mama was off, hurrying behind

So Long for Now

Mr. Harmon, her tap shoes scraping along the concrete as she went.

There was a row of stores across the street from Liberty—a souvenir shop called Philly's Finest, a place that sold candles and stationery, and the takeout restaurant Red called Empanada Pal, because the last three letters of "Palace" had faded from the awning. Even though it was already past six o'clock, the late-June air was still hot and sticky. Empanada Pal's door was flung wide open. Philly's Finest was, too. The lights in both stores were on.

I let go of Teagan's hand, said "Be right back," and made my way to the sidewalk. From there I could see the row houses lined up next door to Liberty. Some of them were worn with age, one of them abandoned. The lights in the row houses were on. I went back to Liberty, to see if its lights had come back on, too.

The building was still dark. Mama and Mr. Harmon were back outside now. He was talking, but Mama didn't seem to be listening. She was looking wildly around, I knew, for me. I hurried over.

"Gabby, you know better than to go off without telling an adult," Mama said.

"I . . . I was just . . . just checking to see if anyone in the houses, um, anyone else had elec—light. If anyone else had lights."

Mama's face and voice softened. "And?" she asked, sounding hopeful.

I nodded my head, already feeling my heart sinking a little. I wasn't sure why, but it seemed bad—really bad—that everyone else had light and Liberty didn't.

"So what does that mean?" Red asked.

"It means we've got a problem on our hands," Mama replied. "And it might be a big one."

My heart sank into my shoes.

That next morning, Saturday, we were back at Liberty to meet Mr. Harmon and Julia Santos. Ms. Santos worked with Mama when Mama needed to get in touch with the city about anything regarding the Liberty building or the grant the city gave us.

When we arrived, Teagan and her grandpa were already there. Mr. Harmon was probably one of the most friendly, upbeat people I knew. He loved sayings, and one of his favorite ones was, *You need clouds to help you appreciate sunshine.* But today he, like Mama, was grim-faced and tight-lipped.

Mama glanced down at her watch. "Ms. Santos and the

building inspector should be here any minute. Let's go inside and wait."

We filed into Liberty to wait for the representatives in the lobby. From there, you could see down almost all of Liberty's hallways, lit up now only by what little sun poured through the windows. Everything looked gray. You could hardly see that the words *Just Dance*, painted on the wall across from the row of dance studios, were not composed of just any old letters. They were composed of tiny pictures of ballet slippers, tap shoes, and music notes, courtesy of Mr. Harmon. You couldn't even really tell that the walls were painted a shade of apple green that had taken Mama three weeks to pick out.

Red walked behind the front desk and tried a light switch. When nothing happened, he came back over to where Teagan and I stood and shrugged weakly. "Just thought something might happen."

For the next few minutes, Mama and Mr. Harmon walked the hallways of Liberty, their chins in their hands, trying light switches just as Red had in hopes, I guessed, that something might happen.

"Do you think the city can fix this in time for the—"

My voice trailed off. Teagan and Red looked away. Neither of them wanted to think about the center not being up and running again in time for Rhythm and Views.

Gabriela

"Anyone here?" a voice called from behind us. "Sorry I'm late."

Ms. Santos was making her way quickly over to the three of us. She was short, red-faced, and wore a full suit even though it was Saturday. A man walked in behind her, carrying a toolbox.

"Hi there," Ms. Santos said. "Are your parents—oh, there they are!"

Mama and Mr. Harmon returned to the lobby. Mama said, "Good to see you again, Julia," to which Ms. Santos replied, "I only wish it was for a different reason. I'm sorry about all this." She asked for a rundown of what had happened the night before.

"Hmmm" was all she said when Mama had finished. "Sounds like it was a dramatic evening. Well, this is Jaime, one of the city's building inspectors. Will you show us the main circuit breaker?"

"Of course."

Mama led the way down the hallway to our right, past the dark, empty dance studios. We came to a stop in front of a door at the end of the hall. Mama took out her master key and unlocked it. The minute the door swung open, I moved in closer for a better look. Red and Teagan did the same. I didn't know what I was hoping to see—maybe one switch turned the opposite direction of all the others. Something easy to fix.

"Gabby?" Mama said.

"Hmmm?" I replied, my focus 100 percent on the circuit breaker.

"Why don't you, Teagan, and Red go wait for us in the lobby?"

"But—"

Mama cocked her head to one side and looked at me. I knew that look. It meant, "Gabriela McBride, do as you're told."

I started back down the hallway, Red and Teagan on my heels. We'd waited in the lobby for what felt like six lifetimes, when the adults' voices became suddenly louder and clearer as they made their way back in our direction. They stopped just short of the lobby. I heard Mama say, "Thank you for coming over here today. We really appreciate it."

The echoes in the hallway and the tap-tap-tapping of Ms. Santos's heels made it so I could only hear some of what she said back to Mama. What I did hear I didn't like one bit: "Building not up to code . . . Unusable . . . Fault."

"Fault?" I said to Teagan and Red, as Ms. Santos and the building inspector breezed by. "*Whose* fault?"

Gabriela

I thought back to the night before, to what had happened right before the lights had gone out. Or, I realized with a sickening lurch of my stomach, what had happened at the *exact moment* everything went pitch-black.

"I-I-It's," I started. "It's . . . our f-f-f-fault."

"You think?" Red asked, his voice shaking.

I nodded miserably. "Th-There wwwwwas—"

Teagan placed her hand on my arm. "What Gabby is trying to say is there was already so much going on at the center. Every room was being used, lights and music on all over the place. And then maybe we . . ." Her voice trailed off. "Maybe Gabby and me were the ones to overload everything when we tried to show our project."

I didn't trust myself to speak, so I just nodded instead. Red looked like he was about to say something, but at that moment, Mama and Mr. Harmon returned to the lobby.

"So what did Ms. Santos say?" I asked. Maybe I'd heard her wrong. "When will the electricity be back on?"

Mama looked at Mr. Harmon. He looked back at her.

"The power is out indefinitely," Mama said.

"All rehearsals and classes are canceled from today on," Mr. Harmon declared. "We can't reenter the building until further notice."

I felt like I'd had the wind knocked out of me. Like the

time I'd fallen during hip-hop rehearsal. One minute I was in the air, doing the same backflip I'd been practicing for months. And the next minute, the floor was rushing up to meet me and there was nothing I could do to stop it.

Mr. Harmon turned to Mama and said, "We'll have to call all the families," and shoved his always-paint-stained hands deep into the pockets of his equally stained khakis.

"I'll take care of that," said Mama. She heaved a huge sigh and turned around, taking Liberty in one last time. "So long, Liberty."

"So long," Mr. Harmon echoed.

As Mama, Red, and I pulled out of the parking lot, I caught a glimpse of the mural Mr. Harmon had been working on a few weeks ago. It was supposed to be these big hearts that told anyone who passed by that Liberty was a building with a lot of love. But Mr. Harmon had only painted the outline of one side of one heart before a freak rainstorm hit that day, leaving just a giant, crooked "C" on the wall. Now who knew how long it would be before the mural was complete?

I took one last look back at Liberty's dark windows and empty parking lot. *So long, Liberty*, I thought. *For now.*

More than Just a Center

Chapter 3

 ama waited for Daddy to come home from work before filling us all in on exactly what Ms. Santos and the inspector had said. Rewiring Liberty would be hugely expensive, and the annual grant we got from the city was not nearly enough to cover the cost.

"We have just enough money to cover salaries as it is," Mama said, resting both hands on either side of her plate.

"But if the city owns the building, why can't they pay for the rewiring?" Red asked.

"Good point," Daddy said. "It seems like this should come out of their budget somewhere." Daddy was a network engineer and, like Teagan, knows all about solving problems.

"Well, Ms. Santos said she will present our case to the city council, but . . ." Mama piled her spoon with chili, brought it to her mouth, and then set the spoon back down. "It's a huge amount of money that we need. She suggested we have the center pay for materials, and the city cover labor expenses."

Rewiring. Hugely expensive. Could Liberty afford to pay for something like that? Mama always said the center wasn't supposed to make her rich. It was supposed to make the community rich—with creativity.

"Did you agree to those conditions?" Daddy prompted Mama gently.

"We agreed to it; Liberty will pay for the materials. But even with that deal in place, Julia said all of this could take time."

"How much time?" Red asked.

Mama's frown deepened. "Not sure."

She ran her hand over her face. *This is all my fault*, I thought. If only Teagan and I hadn't been so obsessed with showing off our surprise. If only we hadn't pressed that big silver button, Liberty would be fine.

"Mama, I . . . I . . . I have something, um, I have something I need to ssssay." I kept my eyes on my chili.

"What is it, Gabby?"

"Thi-Thi-This whole thing . . . thing is . . . it's—" The words were right there, and yet they got stuck, skipping like an old record player. "Never mind." I chanced a question of my own instead. "Are the repairs going to take more than five weeks, four days, and approximately twenty-three and a half hours?"

Daddy laughed, and a smile broke through the mask of worry Mama had been wearing since yesterday.

"It's possible," Mama said. Then added, "Maybe." Her smile began to fade.

Liberty not having Rhythm and Views would be like a Philly cheesesteak without the Whiz. I had to fix what Teagan and I messed up. And maybe if I fixed things fast enough, I wouldn't even need to tell Mama and Daddy that the outage was our fault. "We need to raise money," I said, my mind racing. "We could have a bake sale. Ooh, and sell friendship bracelets. Bria taught me how to make these really pretty ones. And-and—"

Mama smiled again. "Those are great ideas, Gabby, but we're going to need a lot more money than any of those ventures can possibly raise. Listen," she said as my face fell. "A lot has happened today, and I've probably already told you and Red more than I should've. Let's take a break from talking about this for a while, clear our heads?"

But I couldn't clear my head. Not just then. All the worry about the center was making my feet tap like crazy under the table. I headed upstairs to my room as soon as the dinner dishes were cleared. My head was spinning with so many ideas about how to fix Liberty that I practically ran into Red coming out of the bathroom at the top of the stairs.

"Hey, cuz. Look. I'm gonna have a mustache by eighth grade."

Red pointed at one small, thin hair above his lip that had joined the two he'd shown me two weeks ago.

"Congrats," I said flatly, and started stepping around him to get to my room.

Red squinted at me. He had eyes the color of pennies. He was the only one in the family with eyes like that. "You look . . . How can I say this nicely? Like a bottle of soda about to pop."

Was it that obvious? "I'm feeling guilty about . . . You know. Hey—you're not going to tell my mom about how Teagan and I caused the blackout, are you?" I asked.

"Of course not, Gabby!" Red said. "And I mean . . ." He stopped and stared at the floor. "If it's your fault, it's my fault, too. I mean, I turned on all the stage lights for practice, including the spotlight. We probably didn't even need all that stuff, but I wanted it to feel like the real thing, you know?"

I nodded. "Yeah, I know."

Gabriela

Red shook his head. "We've got to fix this."

"But how?" I said.

"Red!" Mama called up the stairs. "Your mother's on the phone!"

Red gave me a nod and then raced down the stairs. I'd run, too, if I only got to talk to my mama a couple times a week.

In my room, I found my cat, Maya, curled up in a little gray-and-white ball in my furry chair, which she'd claimed on the first day we brought her home. I scooped her up and climbed the ladder to my loft bed. We had read Maya Angelou's poem "Life Doesn't Frighten Me" in school last year, right around the time I got Maya. That poem stuck with me—sometimes when I wanted to stop speaking because I was scared someone would laugh at my stutter, I thought about the person in the poem who wasn't afraid of anything.

I sat down beside Maya and said, "What are we going to do about the center?" Maya raised her head and blinked her sleepy, amber eyes.

"Liberty is like another home to me. Do you know I've been going there my whole life? That's ten years, Maya!" I held up all my fingers. "Ten! How am I going to fix this?"

More than Just a Center

In response, Maya stood, stretched, and rubbed her face against my hand.

"You're no help," I said, laughing a little and scratching her behind the ears. She purred and snuggled up next to me, pressing her warm body against mine. For the first time that day, a sense of calm washed over me, the same feeling I got every time I walked into Liberty.

I closed my eyes, picturing the building now. There was an old wind chime hanging above the front door that made everyone's arrival a musical event. When I was little, I used to run in and out, just to hear the chimes tinkle. Liberty is where Teagan and I became best friends, too, and where she and I raced through the hallways, playing tag and hide-and-seek until Stan called out, "Do you two need me to find you something to do? Because Lord knows the moldings need painting and the floors need polishing, too." That was Stan's favorite joke, because Liberty's moldings, though beautiful with curlicues and flower details, were covered in chipping paint and most of its floors were scuffed and scratched beyond repair. Still, for me, being at Liberty was like slipping on my favorite pair of broken-in tap shoes. The center wasn't perfect, but it fit me better than anything.

I knew Stan felt like that, too—he always said the folks

at Liberty were the only family he had. Other people like Mrs. Blake planned their whole weeks around their Liberty classes. Mrs. Blake's husband drove her and waited in his car every Wednesday, reading Shakespeare, while Mrs. Blake learned how to paint.

What would she do without Liberty? What about Amelia? Red? And all the people who depended on the center as a place where they felt at home? To them—and to me—Liberty was something more. It was—I groped around in my mind, searching for the words, but I couldn't pin them down.

I was careful not to disturb Maya as I climbed down to my desk. I took my journal out and turned to a clean page. It took me a few drafts, but I finally had a poem that put my feelings into words.

Liberty is more than just a center
It's us, it's me, it's the heart of all who enter
It's Mr. Harmon, Teagan, Red, Stan, and Mama
It's dance, it's theater, it's art, it's drama
Liberty is where my words can be free
It's us, it's you, it's everyone, it's me

I read the poem aloud a few times, like we did in the poetry group, working on the rhythm. Red said that spoken word poetry goes all the way back to African traditions and can be found throughout many cultures in history. People fighting for civil rights used it to express their anger and stand up for what they believed in. My poem wasn't angry, really, but I sure believed those words. I felt them from the tips of my toes all the way up to my ponytail.

I was reading through once more when Daddy poked his head in my room.

"Gabby?" he said. "It's late. Time to power down."

Daddy seemed to see the world as though it were one big computer. A nap was a chance to reboot; negative thoughts were corrupt files; and family and friends were your network. He told me once how computers shared information by using a data link. I hadn't really understood what he was saying, but he'd kept repeating the word "connected" over and over again.

Connected, like how Liberty connects all of us.

"Daddy!" I said quickly, before he closed the door. "We're a network!"

"Who is, kiddo?" He opened the door and leaned against the doorframe, as Mama and Red came up behind him.

"Liberty."

An idea was forming in my head. I stood up from my desk. "At Liberty, we're all connected like a network! And that's what's most important, the connections we have and all the other—other stuff that we share." I knew that "stuff" wasn't the right word, but I couldn't get my words out fast enough. "What if, until Liberty is fixed, instead of shutting down our network, we moved it someplace else? Just hold classes and rehearsals somewhere else?"

Silence.

I looked from Mama to Daddy to Red.

"W-Well, it seemed like a g-good idea," I muttered, sitting back down.

"It's not a good idea," Mama said. "It's a *great* idea!" She came all the way into my room and began to pace. She only did that when she was really excited about something. "I'll talk to my college dance buddies, see if any of them knows of a studio we can use."

"I'll check in with the guys at work," Daddy added.

"We can ask Principal Stewart if the gym at Thomas Jefferson is free," I said. Red nodded in agreement.

"After all," Daddy said, "one person is only—"

"As strong as his network," we finished in unison. That was one of Daddy's favorite computer metaphors.

Somebody, somewhere was bound to have a space we could use. My heart soared.

More than Just a Center

"All right, you two," Daddy said, "even computers sleep sometimes. How about we humans do the same."

I said good night, brushed my teeth, and climbed into bed, bringing my journal with me. It *was* a good night. I didn't know how we'd raise the money to repair the Liberty building, but with our network held together, I was sure we could do anything.

Network
Linked together
We can weather
Any storm
In any form
Righting the wrong
Million-man-and-woman strong
Ready to fight
Turn darkness back to light

Words and Actions

Chapter 4

On Monday morning, Red and I got up and got dressed, ready to meet Teagan at Thomas Jefferson Elementary to talk to Principal Stewart. Mama had filled in Mr. Harmon yesterday, and Red and I had FaceTimed with Teagan and made a plan to go to the school first thing in the morning. Mama was already downstairs in the kitchen, ending a call on her cell phone.

Daddy looked up from his bowl of cereal. "Who was that?" he asked.

Mama sighed. "One of my senior girls. I left her a voice mail about rehearsal being canceled today. She and the other girls are disappointed, to say the least. This is their last big show at the center before most of them go off to college."

"But the show could still happen, right?" I asked. "Especially if we find another space?"

Words and Actions

Mama took a seat at the table and exchanged a look with Daddy.

"The show could go on," Mama said slowly. "It all depends."

"Depends on what?" Red asked.

"You know, I really don't want you two getting so wrapped up in all of this."

"We just want to know what the show happening depends on," I said.

"Fine. It depends on what the city says and how much money we can raise for materials with other endeavors. Okay? Now that's it. No more questions about this. You two need to enjoy your summer, especially you, Gabby. You start middle school in the fall, which will be a big change for you. I want you to have fun these next couple of months, okay?"

It was not okay. How was I supposed to fix what I messed up if Mama wouldn't even let me ask any questions about it?

"So . . . does asking for a ride to the school count as a question?" Red asked.

"We need to get to TJ to talk to Principal Stewart," I said. The words came out like a stomp in tap class.

"To ask him if Liberty can use the gym," Red reminded her.

Gabriela

Mama frowned. "You two don't need to do that. I'll handle it."

Mama's laptop was open on the kitchen table beside her, and she had a pad of yellow paper in her lap. The top page had a to-do list on it that was very close to reaching the last line on the paper. "See, it's right here on my list." She pointed at number seven.

"But it could be a while before you get to that," I said. "Besides, Red and I want to help because—" I almost said because the outage is our fault, but I stopped myself. I didn't really think Mama would be mad if I told her about pushing the big silver button, but she built the programs at Liberty from the ground up all those years ago and had been working hard ever since. I didn't want to tell her that her own daughter had made it all come crashing down. "Because we want to do as much for Liberty as we can."

Mama's frown deepened. I couldn't understand why she was frowning at all. Couldn't she see how much Red and I wanted to help?

"It was my idea," I said. "Can we please handle it?"

"All right," Mama said at last. "You two can do this one thing. But that's it." Red and I opened our mouths to protest at the same time. Mama held up her hand for silence. "All of what's going on with Liberty is too heavy for you kids to be dealing with. So, yes, you may talk to Principal Stewart. After that, I want you to get on with enjoying your summer. Let the adults do the heavy lifting. Everything is going to work out."

"But we want to—"

Mama's raised hand cut me off again. "I know what you want, and I appreciate all the help you'd like to give, but you need to leave this to the grown-ups." Mama's phone vibrated as a text message came through. "Give me a minute to work through some things on my list and I'll drive you over to TJ."

I went to the living room and sat down heavily on the couch. Red flopped down beside me. It wasn't fair—Liberty was all about community. Weren't Red and I a part of the community, too?

"Mama is treating us like babies," I said miserably.

"Yeah," Red said, punching the couch. "We need to prove that we're not."

"How do we do that?"

"No idea," Red said.

Suddenly, another of Mr. Harmon's favorite sayings popped into my mind: *Prove yourself through your actions, not your words.*

"We have to show Mama that we can handle tough

stuff. Show her that we are, um, capable. That's it. We need to show her that we're capable of doing more."

"How?" Red asked, his voice just as flat as before.

"By doing really well with the job she's letting us do today. If we go to TJ and manage to get Principal Stewart to let us use the gym for the next few weeks, Mama will see that we are capable—"

"And she'll have to let us help out more!" Red put in, already cheering up.

"Exactly."

It turned out that proving yourself is easy to *say* but not actually easy to *do*. Especially when Red and I met up with Teagan outside TJ's main office and the first thing Teagan said was, "Are you ready to talk to Principal Stewart, Gabby?" We had decided the night before on the phone that I would talk to Principal Stewart, which meant that I was going to have to do the exact opposite of Mr. Harmon's quote. I was going to have to prove myself with my words.

"I'm r-ready," I said.

"Are you sure?" Teagan asked.

I nodded.

Principal Stewart was behind the desk in the main

office, writing on the dry-erase board. His back was to us. I stood silently between Teagan and Red, waiting for him to turn around. Teagan elbowed me gently in the ribs. When I looked over at her, she opened her eyes wide and jerked her head in Principal Stewart's direction, as if to say, "What are you waiting for?"

I opened my mouth, then closed it. Mama and Daddy always encouraged me, when I was too nervous to talk to someone, to just take my time and get my words out, stutter and all. I cleared my throat. Principal Stewart turned around to face us, marker still held up as if he were getting ready to scribble a message in the air.

"Good morning," he boomed, and then held up the pointer finger on his free hand. "Wait. Don't tell me. Teagan Harmon?"

Teagan nodded.

"And—"

"Clifford Knight, but everyone calls me Red. I'm up at the middle school."

"Ah, that's why I don't recognize you." Principal Stewart's eyes landed on me. He frowned. School had never been a second home to me the way Liberty was. School was the place where, in fifth grade, Aaliyah Reade-Johnson gave me a nickname that followed me the whole year like a shadow:

"Repeat," because I was always saying stuff more than once. School was where I'd learned to keep my eyes on my desk when the teacher was looking to call on someone to read. Where the same comment appeared on my report card year after year: "Gabby's reluctance to participate in class is negatively impacting her grades." Everyone saw me at Liberty; people hardly noticed me at school.

"Hmmm." Principal Stewart tapped his chin. He frowned. He had no idea who I was. He stared at me, waiting for me to tell him my name. Red stared at me. Teagan did, too.

"Ummmm," I said softly.

"Gabriela McBride," Teagan put in quickly. "Her mom runs Liberty Arts Center."

"Ah yes!" Principal Stewart said so loudly I almost jumped. "First year. Did not quite get to know every name and face."

"And speaking of Liberty . . ." Teagan elbowed me again.

I wished she would stop doing that. And I wished everyone would stop staring at me, too. The inside of my mouth felt like I'd brushed my teeth with sawdust. Principal Stewart glanced at the clock and then back at the dry-erase marker in his hand.

Words and Actions

"W-W-W-We were wondering if, um ... yyyyyyou could like, um. No. Wait. Liberty is in the dark—"

"In the dark?" Principal Stewart cut in. "What do you mean, it's in the dark?"

"I mean ... I mean that it's ... it's ... it's ..." I paused, remembering one of the strategies Mrs. Baxter had taught me to use when my stuttering got out of hand. I took a deep breath and closed my eyes, tried to see the words I wanted to say. I had to pin them down and say them, no matter how they came out. *We had a blackout at Liberty and there's no telling when things will be fixed. So, in the meantime, we need a place to hold classes and rehearsals and were wondering if we could use the gym.*

There. I opened my eyes and my mouth, ready to try again when Teagan chimed in. "What Gabby is trying to say is that this past Friday, the power went out at Liberty. Now the dancers won't be able to rehearse for our Rhythm and Views show at the end of July. We'll also have to stop all the programs at Liberty, like art classes, unless we can find another space to use in the meantime. Which is why we're here this morning: To ask if you'd allow us to use the gym to rehearse for the next few weeks?" Teagan glanced at me. "Sorry," she mouthed.

"It's okay," I mouthed back, trying hard to ignore the feeling in the pit of my stomach.

Gabriela

Principal Stewart rocked back on his heels. "Well, Ms. Harmon, you are some type of orator," he said, letting loose with a laugh like a cannon blast. "Unfortunately, the gym is full-on booked for the next few weeks. I've got summer youth basketball and volleyball in the evenings and junior varsity cheerleading on the weekends. And during the day, the district is using the gym for its Gifted Youth program."

As Principal Stewart ticked each team off on his fingertips, my spirit sank lower and lower.

"But I'll tell you what," he added, checking his watch. "Gifted Youth is in the gym right now for the next fifteen minutes. After that, it's lunch in the caf. I'll walk you down there and see if the director will let the three of you make an announcement of sorts, asking the students in the program if they know of a place you can use to rehearse and whatnot. Sound good?"

"That's a great idea!" Red said.

"It is," Teagan agreed.

I just nodded.

"Great. Off we go then!"

Principal Stewart led the way to the gym. Once inside, we waited on the bleachers while he talked to the director of the Gifted Youth program.

"You're going to do the talking, right, Gabby?" Red asked.

"Yeah."

I still had to prove myself. But as I looked around, I saw the faces of some kids I knew, and a lot I didn't. Some of them looked too big to be in TJ, and a few of them I was certain were already in middle school. My skin grew cold. Beside me, Teagan and Red were saying things like, "Make sure you mention how much Liberty means to the community," and "Tell them how important the show is, too." But I hardly heard them. I was thinking about the time Mrs. Baxter made me write down a list of stuttering triggers, all of the situations that made my stutter worse than usual. Number one on that list was speaking in front of people I didn't know.

"Understandable," Mrs. Baxter had said. *"And now that we've identified that, we can be ready for it."* I wasn't feeling ready now.

Just then, Principal Stewart called the three of us over. "Mr. Ludwig, the director, says it's all right for you to make an announcement. But make it quick, okay?"

And before I knew it, a whistle was blown and all of the members of the Gifted Youth program were sitting on the floor in front of Teagan, Red, and me, waiting for someone to say something. And that someone was me.

Make yourself say the words, Gabby, no matter how they sound, I told myself.

"Um, g-good afternoon . . . noon. My . . . my . . . my name is Gabriela McBride and I . . . I . . . I . . ."

Someone snickered and made a sound like a record skipping. The director rushed to remove the person from the gym. A boy I'd never seen before. My face grew hot and the words I'd planned to say caught in my throat. I cleared my throat, trying to force the words out. But they wouldn't come.

"I'm getting hungry," a boy called out.

"Yeah, me, too," a girl replied.

Hot tears pushed at the back of my eyes. I blinked them away. "Um—" I began.

"Good morning," Teagan cut in. "For those of you who don't know me, I'm Teagan Harmon and I'm here on behalf of the Liberty Arts Center, a place that is as beloved by many of you as it is by me."

I listened as the words I was supposed to say came flowing out of Teagan's mouth. If she'd just given me another few moments, I could've said them myself. Right?

"So we are asking anyone who knows of a place we can

rehearse to please, *please* let us know. That's Gabby McBride, me, Teagan Harmon, and—"

"Red Knight," Red said, stepping forward. "If we don't find a space, we'll be all over the place. So go on and dig deep; we're counting on you, my peeps!"

"Thank you!" Teagan said hurriedly. The Gifted Youth students were already getting to their feet.

Principal Stewart came over to us as the gym emptied out. "Mission accomplished. Why don't the three of you grab some lunch in the cafeteria before you go? Maybe some of the kids are waiting to talk to you already."

"That's a good idea," said Red and Teagan agreed. "Gabby, what do you think?"

I shrugged. I saw Red and Teagan look at each other, then at me. I wished the gym floor would open up and swallow me whole. If we were at Liberty, where we were supposed to be, just like every other Monday, I would've gone to sit in the special place in the auditorium that echoed. But I wasn't at Liberty, couldn't go to Liberty. I felt the tears coming again.

"It's all right, Gabby," said Red, thumping me on the shoulder. "Someone's gonna have a place for us to practice. Liberty's gonna get all fixed up in time for the show, and what happened here? It won't even matter anymore."

Gabriela

I shook my head.

"It doesn't even matter now," Red said. "I bet those kids already forgot. All they were thinking about was lunch. We'll get back into Liberty. We're big-time now, ready for crowds."

"Skyscraper-high," Teagan continued.

Red wriggled his eyebrows at me. I smiled a little, thinking of Liberty up and running again in time for the show.

"Touching clouds," I finished.

Shakespeare and Sandwiches

Chapter 5

Teagan, Red, and I were just sitting down in the cafeteria with our lunch when a boy I'd never seen before plunked his tray down right next to me. I noticed two things about him immediately: He had an Afro at least three inches high, and his lunch box looked more like a red briefcase with a lightning bolt down the middle than any lunch box I had ever seen. We watched, open-mouthed, as he unzipped it and pulled out a thermos and a plastic container.

"Good morrow," he said cheerfully.

"*What?*" said Red.

"Good morrow," the boy repeated, pulling open his plastic container. It had three sections. The largest compartment held a sandwich—the two smaller ones, apple slices and graham crackers. "You're probably wondering why I'm sitting here right now."

Gabriela

"I'm actually wondering about something else," Red replied, eyeing the boy's sandwich. It was cut in the shape of a goldfish.

"I'm here to help. As the Bard once said, ' 'Tis not enough to help the feeble up, but to support him after.' "

"The feeble?" Teagan asked.

"Yes. The weak, the frail." He clenched a fist and dropped his voice to a whisper. "The helpless. In other words, you."

"We're not weak!" I cried.

"Or frail," said Teagan.

"Or helpless," said Red.

The boy took a bite of his goldfish-shaped sandwich. "No," he said around a mouthful of turkey and cheese. He sounded a little disappointed. "I guess you're not. But that's one of my favorite quotes by the Bard."

"Okay," said Red, putting his milk down on the table. "Exactly *who* is this Bard you keep talking about?"

"William Shakespeare," the boy answered. "The greatest writer and poet who ever lived."

"The *greatest*?" Red cocked his head to the side. "I heard they use Shakespeare to torture kids in high school. Nah, if you wanna talk the greatest poet, you need to be talking about Langston Hughes. Maya Angelou. And the best spoken word poet today, Saul Williams."

The boy shrugged. "They're all great, true, but Shakespeare came first. Anyway, my name is Isaiah Jordan and, like I said, I'm here to help. You say you need a place to practice for your show; my dad's church happens to have a rec room you might be able to use. It's Mount Calvary Baptist."

"Are you serious?" I asked.

"Um, yeah."

"How soon will you know if we can use the room?" I was so excited my words burst out of me like a racehorse.

"I'll ask my dad tonight. Give me your number and I'll call you and tell you what he says."

I couldn't believe it. We'd only just expanded our network and already things were looking up!

As soon as Red and I got into the car that afternoon, I spilled the big news to Mama. I couldn't get the story out fast enough, telling her all about asking Principal Stewart, the announcement in the gym, and ending with Isaiah's offer. I stopped talking long enough to take a breath and

Gabriela

Mama said, "Why didn't you make the announcement, Gabby?"

Of all the questions I expected Mama to ask, that was *not* one of them. "I don't know. I mean, um, you know why," I muttered.

Mama pulled into our driveway, and the three of us went inside. Daddy was still at work; the house was quiet and dark. Mama led us into the kitchen and started washing off pieces of fruit.

"So," she began, her voice trailing off.

"It'll be awesome if Isaiah's dad says yes," I said.

"Oh, absolutely," Mama agreed. "One of the guys at your father's job might have a place, too, just in case things with your friend don't work out." She paused. "Gabby, did you try to use the techniques Mrs. Baxter taught you?"

I groaned. "I tried, but I couldn't do it, so Teagan jumped in to help."

Mama's face softened. "And how do you feel about that?"

"Fine," I said, but that feeling in the pit of my stomach was back again, only stronger this time. *You're annoyed at yourself for freezing up because that boy snickered*, I thought. A little, that was true. But that wasn't all of it. I was annoyed at Teagan, too, for jumping in with Principal Stewart *and* with the announcement in the gym. If I'd just taken another few seconds, visualized the words in my head and then pinned them down—I could've been the one to speak up both times for Liberty. I knew in my heart that Teagan was just trying to support me, so I pushed the feeling away.

"I'm fine with it," I said again, just as my phone rang. I picked it up immediately. "Hello?"

"How fares, my lady?"

"I'm sorry, what?"

"It's Isaiah. 'How fares, my lady?' is Shakespearean lingo for 'how are you?' "

"Oh. Okay."

Pause.

"So?" Isaiah said.

"So, what?" I replied.

"How are you?"

"Fine. What did your dad say about the rec room?" I blurted out, realizing only after I'd spoken how rude I sounded. "Sorry," I quickly added, catching Mama's disapproving look. "We're just really, um, like—" I groped around for the right word.

"Anxious," Red supplied.

"Anxious," I said.

"I get it. Well, my father said yes. You can use the rec room at our church free of charge for rehearsals or whatever you need it for until Liberty is back to its old self again."

I let out a whoop. "Starting when?"

"As soon as you're ready."

"Thank you, thank you, thank you!"

"Hang on," Mama said. "I'd like to speak to his father."

I asked Isaiah to get his father on the phone, then handed my phone over to Mama. She carried it into the living room. I could hear Mama saying, "Thanks. And the dimensions are . . . I see. That sounds like it might work. Do you have any pics you can send me?"

"Sounds like she wants to use the space," I whispered.

Red was beaming. We'd done it. We'd shown Mama we could help fix Liberty. We had found a place for rehearsals, which meant we'd be ready for Rhythm and Views. Mama and Mr. Harmon could still teach their classes, too. This was the lightest I'd felt since Saturday, so light that I jumped up from my chair and did a tuck jump right there in the kitchen. Red laughed.

"How do you even *do* that?" he asked. "It's like you have wings."

At that moment, I felt like I had wings, too. Maybe I hadn't presented our case to Principal Stewart or made the announcement in the gym, but I'd played a part in helping us find a temporary home for our Liberty family. And that counted for something.

"Victory," Red said to me as we set the table for dinner a little while later.

It would be leftovers that night—Mama and Daddy, who'd just come in from work, were at the computer, coming up with a schedule for rehearsals and classes starting next week in the rec room.

"Victory," Red repeated thoughtfully. "Feels like crossing the finish line." He looked at me, raised his eyebrows.

"You want *me* to—"

"Yup."

"Okay. Victory feels like crossing the finish line. It . . . it . . . um . . . um—oh, I don't know. I'm not as good at this as you are!"

"And I'm not as good at jumping eighteen feet in the air with pointed toes, but I'll try if it makes you feel better."

"Red, you don't have to—"

But Red had already put down the handful of paper napkins he was holding and was airborne. He twisted wildly in midair, landed a foot away from his starting point, and lost his balance. He crashed to the floor, knocking over the garbage can in the process.

"What's going on in there?" Mama called.

Gabriela

I could hardly get my words out since I was laughing. "Nothing," I gasped.

I laughed until hot tears pricked at the corners of my eyes. Until I thought my chest would burst. Red got to his feet, a smile plastered on his face. "So like I was saying, I *know* you can rhyme better than I can leap. So try it. What does victory sound like? Look like? Taste like?"

"*Taste* like?" I wiped at my eyes.

"Yeah. Taste like."

I thought for a moment. "Victory feels like crossing the finish line. It tastes sweet like Key lime pie."

"Looks like the show going on in the final hour."

"Sounds like Liberty, lights on, full power."

Shoulder to Shoulder, Chest to Chest

Chapter 6

Mama and Mr. Harmon needed some time to get organized at Mount Calvary, so Teagan, Red, and I had a lot of time to "enjoy our summer" that week. If it were any other summer, Teagan and I would have been hanging out at Liberty exploring old crawl spaces, or helping Mama or Mr. Harmon in their classes. Today, we were sitting on the back porch, making friendship bracelets to sell to raise money for Liberty. I knew it would take thousands and thousands of bracelets to cover the repairs, but I couldn't just sit around and do nothing. Not when people like Stan and Mrs. Blake counted on Liberty. I wondered what they were doing today.

The screen door flew open. "What're you up to, cuz, and

cuz's friend who wears a beanie even in the summer-time?"

I jumped up off the steps so fast, I knocked our box of embroidery thread halfway across the yard. "Red, you scared me!"

"And no one ever said beanies are only for the winter!" Teagan cried.

"Sorry," Red replied. "But really, what are you doing?"

"We *were* making bracelets," I said.

Red peered down at our efforts so far. "No Eagles' or Phillies' colors?" He shook his head. "Good thing I came out here, huh? We can make some in the team colors and ask Philly's Finest to sell them for us."

That actually wasn't a bad idea.

Red sat down while Teagan got him some thread. Then she showed him how to tie the knots. A few minutes later, all three of us were sitting quietly, concentrating on our bracelets. The weaving of the colors reminded me of Liberty's stained glass. It was about noon, so there wouldn't be a ton of colored light on the worn floors—just some over by the heaters in studio seven.

Through the screen door came the sound of Mama's voice. She was in the kitchen, talking to someone on her cell phone.

"Please tell her this is the fourth message I've left," Mama said. "Yes, Tina McBride, regarding the Liberty Arts building repairs. Thank you."

There was silence for a few moments, and then Mama said, "Hi, Louis. Yes, the girls are just fine. I'm calling to tell you that I still haven't heard from Julia. She hasn't responded to any communication yet. Not even to the e-mail I sent her about the Dream Together campaign."

Red and I looked at each other. We didn't know they'd started an online fund-raising effort. Teagan pulled out her phone and silently found the page. They hadn't raised much money yet.

"Yes," Mama was saying now. That probably couldn't hurt . . . How about I . . ." Her voice faded as she left the kitchen.

"I can't believe they didn't tell us they started this Dream Together campaign!" I said as soon as Mama was out of earshot. "We could've been spreading the word about that this whole week!"

"Seriously," Red said. "We've been good about not asking too many questions—" He turned to Teagan. "Trying to give Aunt Tina some space and all that—but we still want to know what's going on, even though they're all, 'leave it to the grown-ups.'"

"My grandpa's been saying the same thing," Teagan said miserably. "He says 'Kids should have a summer, not be all wrapped up in adults' business. Why in my day, all I knew about my father's auto body shop was how to unclog the customer toilet.' "

"Ew," I said.

"Tell me about it," Teagan replied.

Mama wandered back into the kitchen. "Sounds great, Louis. I think this could work. Would you like to join us for lunch? We can tell them about it then." A pause. "Yes, about the show, too. See you soon."

I didn't know what Mama and Mr. Harmon were planning to tell us over lunch, but suddenly I was very hungry.

"So," Mama started, placing a pitcher of lemonade on the picnic table. "We wanted to ask you all something." She eyed Mr. Harmon.

"You kids know we've been waiting to hear back from Ms. Santos about how the city wants to handle the repairs," Mr. Harmon said. We all nodded. "Well, neither of us have heard a peep from her since she left Liberty last Saturday. We're beginning to worry that Liberty could fall through the cracks at the city offices."

Shoulder to Shoulder, Chest to Chest

Fall through the cracks? How could a whole building—a whole community—fall through the cracks? Mama ran her hand over her face. She was wearing a bracelet I'd made—purpley magenta, like my costume for the opening number of Rhythm and Views. I realized with a start that the show was exactly four weeks away. If the city didn't come through, it didn't matter how many friendship bracelets we made. Liberty wouldn't be up and running again and there would be no show. Tiny tap dancers started tapping in my chest.

"So," Mama said again, placing both hands flat on the table. "We're thinking of having a rally next Sunday, out in front of the Liberty building, something to get the city's atten—"

"I'm there, Aunt Tina! We're all there! Just tell us what we can do to help!"

"Yeah!" Teagan and I echoed. Teagan was already reaching for Cody and a pen.

"Hold on," Mama said. "Let me finish. We're thinking the rally will get people's attention . . ." She looked at Mr. Harmon.

"And then we'll ask them to sign a petition to show their support for Liberty."

I liked the sound of that.

Mama continued. "We figure we'll need at least two hundred signatures. We can also hand out postcards with the Dream Together info on them—"

"Thanks for telling us about that, by the way," I interrupted, and then immediately said, "Sorry. I-I-It's just that we like to knnnnnow what's going on with Liberty."

"I know you do, Gabby," Mama said. "That's why we're looping you in now. And we've been impressed with your bracelet efforts this past week. If we set up a table, would you sell them at the rally?"

That was something—Mama was at least asking us to help a little bit. "Of course," I said. Red and Teagan agreed. But bracelets only made a difference if we got the city's attention. Maybe this was our chance to do something more for Liberty, do something to right our wrong.

"What about the petitions?" I asked. "Can we help with those? A few of the poetry kids could have clipboards ready and we could grab people to sign the petition as they go by." I sat up straighter to show I was serious about helping. Red and Teagan did, too.

Mama and Mr. Harmon did that thing where grown-ups talk to each other without talking at all. They just used their eyebrows and stuff. They nodded.

Shoulder to Shoulder, Chest to Chest

One week and one day from today, I would have the chance to really make a difference for Liberty.

Shoulder to shoulder
Chest to chest
On Germantown Avenue
Shouting
Telling everyone that Liberty is the best!
Our voices will carry
Across the street, the city
The state, the planet
Our love for Liberty will never vanish
Shoulder to shoulder
Chest to chest
On Germantown
Is where we'll be
Praising Liberty

In a New Space

Chapter 7

 onday was our first day at Mount Calvary Baptist, and I couldn't wait to dance again—all those bracelets had made my body stiffer than a pair of Amelia's brand-new pointe shoes. Mama, Red, and I met Mr. Jordan in the parking lot, and he walked us into the rec room. I gasped before I could stop myself.

The room was huge, but everything in it was gray and sharp. The walls were painted a silver gray, except for one, which was the brightest shade of yellow I'd ever seen. Even the hardwood floors were gray, the borders around the sparkling windows, *and* the futuristic chairs that looked like the hollowed-out halves of hard-boiled eggs. There weren't any mirrors on the walls, just different black-and-white pictures of Philadelphia's skyline.

"Completely redone," Mr. Jordan said proudly. He had

an Afro just like Isaiah's. "As modern as modern can get. Virtually flawless."

Liberty was full of what Mr. Jordan would probably think were flaws and outdated things like the phone niche in studio seven. How would I spot without that?

There wasn't any stained glass in the windows, but the sunlight that came through them was bright and buttery. It pooled on the floor the same way it did at Liberty, and I had to admit, the futuristic chairs *did* look kind of cool. Plus, a few days before, Daddy and Mr. Harmon had rented a van to bring over some of the equipment from Liberty, like the ballet barre and artists' easels. So even though the rec room wasn't Liberty, a little bit of the center had made its way to Mount Calvary Baptist Church.

Mama thanked Mr. Jordan and he disappeared back upstairs. "Time to get down to business," she said to Red and me. Mama had booked Tiny Tots, Mr. Harmon's art class, *and* my make-up rehearsal with Amelia. "The space is big enough," she'd said.

But we soon learned that only a football field would have been big enough. The Tots were all over the place moments after they arrived. I ran around, trying to help Mama collect them.

"Oh, honey, don't," I heard Mrs. Blake say to one of the

little girls. She was gently prying a container of paint from the girl's small hands.

"Taylor, over here," Mama said, calling the Tot back. And then, "Where is Louis?" Mama whipped out her phone and called Mr. Harmon. She hung up moments later, looking positively panicked. "He said he never got the e-mail with the new sched—"

A crash sounded from across the room. I looked up in time to see an easel on its side and Red running over to calm Mrs. Blake, who was fanning herself with her hand.

"Is Louis coming today, Tina?" Mrs. Blake said loudly and then, "Oh, oh, honey. *Don't!* You'll get paint on your—"

Too late. While Mrs. Blake was busy asking Mama about Mr. Harmon, Taylor had succeeded at last in opening the jar of paint. Her once crisp white tutu was now streaked with blobs of turquoise. Taylor spun around happily, shouting, "I'm blue, I'm blue!"

"Technically, you're cerulean," Mrs. Blake said miserably.

Mama groaned.

"Tag," another Tiny Tot yelled jubilantly, and darted off in the other direction.

"No! Not tag!" I shouted. "Red, help!"

Red joined in, and by the time Mama was done wiping

In a New Space

Taylor down, we'd managed to get the Tiny Tots collected and sitting in a restless, giggly circle. I was panting and sweaty. Red was, too.

"Louis never got the e-mail with the rec center schedule," Mama said, rubbing her temples. "I'm going to have to run Tots *and* figure out what to do with the art class. I don't want them to feel like they wasted their time."

"Don't worry," Red declared. "I'm on it."

Mama opened her mouth to protest, but Red had already strutted over to the women sitting at their easels and said loudly, "Good morrow, ladies. May I entertain you with some free verse poetry?"

Mama stared at Red, open-mouthed, and then turned to me.

"We should get those rally posters hung up in here," she said. "And the sign-up sheets for shifts at the info table. Would you mind doing that?"

"Of course, Mama." She pointed me toward the posters and a roll of tape, and I headed to the front door to hang one there.

Suddenly, the door swung open, almost smacking me in the face.

"Just who I was looking for," Amelia said. "Ready

for that make-up rehearsal?" She tapped me on the nose the way she did sometimes to say hi, or when I forgot something. "What're those?" she asked, gesturing to the posters.

I explained about the rally.

"Sounds like fun, actually," Amelia said. "Count me in. Now let's get dancing—less than four weeks to the show." She raised her eyebrows, a hopeful look on her face. "If it's still happening?"

"I think so," I said. Or at least I hoped. I'd started getting this feeling in my stomach, heavy like my tap shoes, whenever I thought about Rhythm and Views. Mama hadn't said anything, but it was getting harder and harder to believe Liberty would be fixed in time for the show.

"Good," said Amelia, but her face said she had heavy tap shoes in her belly, too. Amelia had been an apprentice director with the Liberty Dance Company for a year and a half. She was twenty-three and one of the best dancers I'd ever seen, and a great teacher, too. I knew how badly she wanted to see her students perform. If only we hadn't pressed that silver button . . .

"Gabby?" Amelia was already facing me, her hand

resting lightly on the barre. "Is everything okay? You look like someone kidnapped your cat."

"Y-Y-Yes," I stammered. "I'm ffffffine."

"Okay," Amelia said slowly. "Let's do some quick pliés. After that we can run through what you missed."

I quickly slipped on my ballet shoes and placed my hand on the barre at the front of the room, trying to push the outage at Liberty out of my mind. We did arch presses and then moved into demi-pliés. We were on second position when Amelia sighed. "It's just not the same here, is it?"

I didn't answer. It felt as if the air around me weighed a hundred tons. Just as some part of me wanted to tell Mama I had caused the outage so I could apologize, part of me wanted to tell Amelia, too. She'd only been at Liberty a couple years, but I couldn't imagine Liberty without her. I moved into fourth position.

"Wait, no, Gabby, you skipped third position," Amelia corrected. I moved to third position and continued just as Taylor and another Tiny Tot abandoned their class.

"Hi, Amelia Bedelia!" they said, dissolved into giggles, and ran away.

"Hi, girls," Amelia replied. "Good, Gabby, now fifth

position. Wait. No. Fourth. Sorry. Looks like this place has got us both all turned around."

Amelia was what Mama called a "born ballet dancer." She was so graceful, her movements so fluid, she could make climbing the stairs look like a move from *Swan Lake*. But tonight, there was something slow and forced about the way she did her pliés, as if her arms and legs were filled with sand. I knew it was because we weren't in studio four at Liberty, the one she liked the best because of the old-fashioned dancer's mirror. The mirror was nearly eight feet tall with a thick black frame covered in painted vines. It was still there because it was too heavy to move, but Amelia said she hoped it stayed forever. "It reminds you that ballet has history."

Amelia cared about Liberty just as much as me.

"A-A-A-Amelia, there's something . . . something I n-n-need to, um, to tell you."

"What is it?"

"Um, well. It's that it's that, I, um—"

I looked up at Amelia. She wasn't like that kid at TJ, who'd laughed when I stuttered. She was looking back at me, her face full of concern as she waited patiently for me to say words she probably wouldn't want to hear in the end. Words I still wasn't ready to say.

In a New Space

"I . . . I . . . I found this place. With Teagan and . . . and Red."

"Did you? Not bad, Gabby," she said, tapping me on the nose again. "I must admit, I *am* digging that yellow wall and those chairs. So, ready to dance?"

I nodded. I would apologize for causing the blackout another time.

Poetry, Paint, and Pliés
Chapter 8

That Friday, the poetry group met for the first time (so did Amelia's senior ballet girls and Mr. Harmon's Art in Your Heart class). Red and I expected to see Bria, Alejandro, and Teagan with their poetry notebooks, but instead we found Teagan with Isaiah and Mr. Jordan, standing side by side near the egg chairs. Mr. Jordan wore a full three-piece suit and copper-colored shoes shinier than a brand-new penny. Isaiah wore a T-shirt that read *Prose Before Bros.*

"Hello there!" Mr. Jordan declared. He had the kind of voice you could hear across state lines.

"Hi," Red and I said together. "Hi, Isaiah. Hi, Teagan," I added.

Isaiah waved shyly. I noticed he wasn't acting anything

like the bold kid who'd sat down at our lunch table two weeks ago. He was staring down at the floor.

"Mr. Jordan wanted to ask about the poetry group," Teagan said. She couldn't take her eyes off of Mr. Jordan. With his inches-high Afro, he appeared to be about seven feet tall.

"I asked your mother about the programs earlier this week, and when she told me you all get together and write poems, I thought that'd be perfect for my boy, Isaiah," Mr. Jordan said. "Why, he's a regular Shakespeare." Isaiah barely made it to his father's elbow. When Mr. Jordan clapped Isaiah on the back for emphasis, Isaiah's knees buckled.

"Dad, come on," Isaiah muttered, rubbing his shoulder.

"Don't be modest," Mr. Jordan said. Then he dropped his voice to a whisper that was surely loud enough to be heard in South Jersey. "And this is a good opportunity for you to make some friends before you start at the public school this year."

Isaiah looked like he wanted to bolt from the room.

"So, what do you say?" Mr. Jordan asked Red, Teagan, and me.

"Sure, we'd love it if Isaiah joined," I said.

"Absolutely," said Red and Teagan.

Gabriela

"Outstanding," Mr. Jordan boomed. "I'll be in my office when you're all done, okay, Isaiah? Don't forget about your snack." He pointed at Isaiah's lunch box, resting on one of the chairs.

Isaiah nodded. And just like that, Mr. Jordan was gone, leaving a cloud of cologne behind him.

"Look," Isaiah said as soon as his father disappeared through the rec room door, "you guys don't have to let me join if you don't want to. It's just that my dad is obsessed with me making friends, and I'm not really fitting in with the Gifted Youth kids. Sure they're youth, but gifted? Would you believe they've never heard of any of Shakespeare's plays besides *Romeo and Juliet*?"

I could believe it, but I didn't say so. I knew what it was like not to fit in. Thanks to my stutter, I felt like an outsider whenever I was around anyone who wasn't part of my family.

"You can join our group," I said, looking around for Bria and Alejandro, "especially now that it looks like we're missing a couple members."

As if on cue, Bria and Alejandro came bursting through the rec room doors.

"Sorry we're late!" They sat down quickly, eyeing Isaiah, who'd opened up his lunch box and pulled out something wrapped in aluminum foil. I looked at Red and Teagan. They looked back at me. Isaiah smiled widely at Alejandro and Bria and said, "Good-e'en, good fellows!"

"I'm sorry, what?" Bria said.

"It means 'good evening' in Shakespearean."

"Oh," Bria replied. "Are you new?" She was talking to Isaiah, but looking around the rec room, taking in all the action. Alejandro did the same.

"Isaiah's dad runs this church. Isaiah's going to join our poetry group, if you guys don't mind," I said.

"It's cool," Bria said, her eyes still raking over the room.

"Yeah, no problem," Alejandro said. "Do you have poems already?"

Isaiah had unwrapped the small aluminum foil–covered bundle. "Do I have poems already?" he said. "Is this sandwich shaped like a star?"

It was.

"Um, cool," Bria said. "So how's it going in this new space so far?"

Red, Teagan, and I exchanged a look.

"My tap shoes sound great on this floor," I said, leaving out that I kept messing up during all of my rehearsals because I didn't have my phone niche to use as a spot.

"My grandfather said the lighting here is great!"

Gabriela

Teagan added. She wasn't entirely honest, either. Mr. Harmon *had* said that the light in the rec room was great, but he'd also said the light in his studio at Liberty was infinitely better.

"Yeah, it's been great," said Red, standing and clapping his hands loudly. "So, welcome and all that. Since it's been a minute and we're in this new place, I thought we could just catch up with some new poetry and move rehearsal for Rhythm and Views to next time. Gabby and I can start us off with a new poem."

"We can?" I asked.

"Yeah. Let's talk about victory."

"Um . . ."

At Liberty, we usually used studio six for poetry club meetings. We'd lie out in a circle on the hardwood floor. It was the smallest of the studios, but it worked for us because it felt like our words would stay in that little room with us, safe. Here, things were different. Our words were out in the open. But I had helped find this place, so I had to show everyone else it was okay.

I caught Amelia's eye across the room as she directed her students. She tapped her nose real quick. "And . . . plié, relevé!"

I got slowly to my feet.

"Th-Th-This is a first dr-dr-draft," I said.

"First draft!" everyone said together. Well, everyone except Isaiah. He was smart, though. He would join in next time. We'd been doing this since we started the poetry group. I loved the boost of confidence it gave me, but today, I noticed a few kids from Mr. Harmon's class leaning around their easels. Mr. Harmon called them back to attention. Maybe we'd have to make a new rule and whisper "first draft" from now on.

Red started. "Victory feels like crossing the finish line."

I took a deep breath and went on, trying not to imagine everyone in the whole rec room hearing my words. I tried to focus only on the poetry kids, two people who were family to me and two people who had become my good friends in this special group. "Tastes sweet like . . . like K-K-K-Key lime pie."

"Looks like the show going on in the final hour."

"Ssssssounds like Liberty, l-l-lights on, full power."

The group clapped, and I cringed inside. Mr. Harmon had to call his students to order yet again. "Thank you, thank you, still a work in progress," Red said as I returned to my seat. "Anyone else—"

"On those tippy-toes, ladies!" came Amelia's voice.

Red went up on his tippy-toes and raised his hands over his head.

"And plié again," said Amelia.

Red dropped down into a too-deep plié and almost toppled over. We all laughed. "I've got another poem," he said from his squatting position on the floor. "A short one, inspired by real events. This is a first draft."

"Wait!" I said. "Let's all whisper 'first draft,' so we don't bother the other students."

"Not sure that's going to have the same effect," Alejandro said, "but I'll try anything once."

Red nodded at me and then looked to the group. "This is a first draft."

"First draft," we all whispered, Isaiah included. It wasn't awful.

"It's called 'Paint on a Tutu' and it goes a little something like this:

"Little girls and old ladies
Paint and easels
This could get crazy
Little girls, they zig, they zag
A jar of blue paint
This is gonna be bad!
Pop goes the lid, now everything's blue
The old lady and the little girl's tutu

Poetry, Paint, and Pliés

All this and only the first day
But we'll make it work at Mount Calvary."

I laughed along with everyone else. Only Red could take our first chaotic day in the new space and turn it into a hilarious poem. Once he got everyone going, Teagan stood up to share a poem she'd been working on since the last time we'd met. Then Alejandro went. Bria was the last to volunteer.

"I might want to use this one for the show, but I wanted you guys to hear it first," she said, and stood. "It's a first draft."

"First draft!" we whispered.

"Okay. It's called—"

"Allongé, Brittney. Elongate those limbs." Amelia's voice cut in again.

Red stretched his leg in front of him and pointed his toe. Bria smiled and then began again. "It's called 'Home,' and it's about how I moved into a new house this year and I miss my old one. But it can kind of relate to us being here instead of Liberty, too. All right, here goes.

"Home is a warm bowl of soup
Just right, like my grandma used to make—"

Gabriela

"Move downstage. That's right, now piqué turn."

Bria frowned. Red jumped to his feet and spun a quick turn, but Bria didn't laugh. She went on, her voice a little flatter than before.

"Crackers sprinkled on top, hold the green
        peppers, hold the carrots
Hold my memories and me
Like home—"

"I don't want to see rounded shoulders, ladies. Stand up straight and tall."

"Forget it," Bria muttered, and sat back down.

"But you were doing great," I said.

"You were," Teagan agreed.

Bria shook her head. "Just forget it. It's almost time to go anyway. I'm going to go outside and wait for my dad."

"Me, too," said Alejando. Scraping chairs and easels plowed over his words.

Alejandro shook his head.

They pushed their way out of the rec room through the crowd of dancers and art students. Teagan, Red, and I looked at one another, and I wondered if they were thinking the same thing as me: The rec room wasn't working. At all.

Poetry, Paint, and Pliés

Isaiah said, "I bid you all adieu," and went upstairs to find his father. As Red and I made our way over to Mama, and Teagan went over to her grandfather, I bumped into Brittney, a tall senior dancer with a braided bun and glasses.

"Sorry," I said.

Brittney glared at me and stalked off.

"What was that about?" Red asked.

"I don't know."

I watched Brittney leave. She made it to the door before a thought occurred to me and my stomach filled with ice. What if she and the other dancers knew the outage was my fault?

Network Repairs

Chapter 9

That night, as soon as we got home from Mount Calvary, I trudged upstairs to my room, Maya on my heels. She joined me on my bed and began to pace back and forth, meowing. I rubbed the patch of white fur on her chest and said, "We found the rec room, but now the rec room isn't working, Maya, and—"

I wasn't sure I was ready to say what I had to say next, not even to Maya. She looked up at me and meowed again.

"If I tell you, you promise you won't tell anyone else?"

Maya rubbed her cheek against my hand and purred. "Well, I think—I think other people may suspect that Red, Teagan, and I may have caused the outage."

Saying this aloud didn't make me feel any better. In fact, guilt pressed down on me heavier than before, like a big, bulky sweater I couldn't shrug off.

Network Repairs

"What am I going to do, Maya?"

Ever since the outage at Liberty, I had so much inside me that I wanted to say but couldn't. I wanted to tell everyone—especially Mama, Amelia, and Mr. Harmon—that the outage was our fault. I wanted to tell Bria how sorry I was that she didn't get to share her whole poem. Somehow I felt like that was my fault, too.

I gave Maya one last good belly rub, climbed down off my bed, and went over to my desk, hoping a new poem might help me clear my head. The Answer, I wrote at the top of the page.

I thought the answer was a gray room
With gray chairs
And one yellow wall
Because community isn't about a space
Or a place
It's about people coming together, sharing
Two dancers in one mirror
Two brushes in one jar of paint
Zillions of words coming together
To make
One conversation
One poem

Gabriela

One space, a shared place
But the gray room is
One dancer glaring at another
Too many conversations
Zillions of words crashing together
Louder than Broad Street Station
The real answer is on Germantown Ave
In a building made of brick
Where sunlight makes puddles of color
On dance floors
Worn and scratched from years of feet moving
Grooving
Tapping
Stomping
Liberty
The place we need to be
To rebuild our community

I read it again and again, and each time the same words jumped up and shouted out me: *Rebuild our community.*

"What you up to, cuz?"

I leapt out of my desk chair so fast it toppled over onto its side. Maya came flying down off my bed and went tearing from the room, her tail lashing wildly. "Red, you've got to stop doing that!"

"Sorry. I knocked; you were so into your diary or whatever you didn't hear."

I righted my chair and sat back down. "It's not a diary. It's a journal and sometimes I write poems in it."

Red leaned against my desk. "Did you write a new one just now?" When I nodded, Red asked, "What about?"

"Liberty and how the rec room isn't a good replacement for it. It's not helping us rebuild our community."

"Yeah, I know." Red leaned his head against the leg of my bed, his body curving over.

I stared at him. There was something about the C shape Red was making with his body. Something familiar, but I couldn't quite put my finger on it. I closed my eyes and racked my brain. Suddenly, I realized what looked so familiar. The shape Red had created was the same shape as Mr. Harmon's unfinished mural on the wall at Liberty.

An idea popped into my head like fireworks. "Th-The mural," I said. Red snapped out of his thoughts and sat up straight. "We can invite people from the center to finish it together at the rally—if that's okay with Mr. Harmon. People are starting to forget why Liberty's so great—"

Gabriela

"—but this could remind them what we're working toward together!" Red finished. "It's a great idea, cuz." He offered his hand for a high five.

"I guess we have to ask Mr. Harmon? And Mama?" I said. "And we'll have to get the word out tomorrow since the rally's on Sunday."

"Yeah," Red said. "You text Teagan; I'll ask Aunt Tina."

"Deal," I said.

The mural might not actually do anything to help us get back into the Liberty building, but it might help repair our network. We would be stronger together.

Rallying

Chapter 10

Mama and Mr. Harmon were on board for the mural, but made it clear they were counting on us for the petitions and bracelets. That made me a little sad and annoyed at the same time—the mural was *my* idea. But I had volunteered for the petitions and I wanted to show Mama I could follow through. Bria was going to run the bracelet sales.

The morning of the rally, Mama, Daddy, Red, and I arrived at 8:30 a.m. to set up. The sky was bright blue, streaked with ribbons of white clouds. Being back at Liberty for the first time in two weeks made me feel like I was up on those clouds, floating.

"Motherboard to Monitor," Daddy called out, grinning. That's what he always said when he wanted to get my or

Red's attention. "Enough staring up at the sky. We've got work to do."

Mr. Harmon laid down his tarps and set up his paintbrushes and paint on the sidewalk in front of the mural while Mama and Daddy set up two tables: one with info on Liberty and the campaign, and one with all our bracelets. Red, Teagan, Isaiah, and I each took a clipboard and a stack of petitions. At the top of the forms was the "appeal" Mama had come up with:

> *On June 23, 2017, the power failed at the heart of our community, Liberty Arts Center. So far, the city's Parks and Recreation Department is not making the needed repairs a priority. We know what Liberty means to the community and how much we all want it back up and running. To show the Parks and Recreation Department that you stand with Liberty, please sign this petition.*

Soon, Bria, Alejandro, and Amelia arrived. I tapped my own nose and waved across the parking lot as Amelia made her way to help Mr. Harmon with the mural. Beside me, Teagan was handing Isaiah and Alejandro clipboards, too.

"Okay," she said in her businesslike voice. "Remember:

Rallying

This is a busy street. People are going to be rushing to one place or another. They're not going to necessarily have time to hear this whole thing." She pointed at the long, italicized paragraph on the top of the page. "So I've come up with a nice shortened version."

I'd already heard Teagan's shortened version multiple times. In fact, I couldn't quite shake the feeling that she was repeating it so many times for my benefit. *She's worried that I'll stutter and mess things up*, I thought.

"Gabby?"

"Huh?"

"What's wrong?"

Teagan was staring at me. So was everyone else.

"Nothing's wrong. Why?"

"You have this look on your face, like, I don't know—"

"Like you just realized your treacherous uncle was responsible for your father's death."

Now we all stared at Isaiah. He sighed. "Has no one read *Hamlet*?"

"No, Isaiah, we haven't," I replied. "And there's nothing wrong with me."

"If you say so," Teagan said, adjusting her beanie with her free hand. "Are you all good with what to say?"

Annoyance bubbled up in me like lava. "Yes, I am," I

said as calmly as I could. "I'm going to go see if your grandfather needs any help."

I moved away and around the corner out of Teagan's sight. The truth was, I *was* nervous about having to go up and talk to strangers. I didn't know why I volunteered for a petition shift. I just knew I wanted to help in whatever way I could. I took a deep breath and, after checking to make sure Teagan was nowhere near her grandfather, went over to where Mr. Harmon stood, hands on hips, gazing at the unfinished mural.

"I think I'm going to let everyone pick his or her own color paint," he said. "And just add on to the mural however they like. Many colors coming together to create one piece of art. What do you think?"

"Sounds perfect," I said. As Mr. Harmon talked, I felt a little of my annoyance disappear.

Now that we had everything set up, it was time to get all eyes on Liberty. Mama, Daddy, and a few of Liberty's regulars held up signs Mr. Harmon had made for them that said things like SAVE LIBERTY! Even Stan showed up wearing his same old navy-blue janitor pants. He held a sign that said, DON'T LET THEM KEEP LIBERTY IN THE DARK! When I caught his eye, he winked at me and waved.

Rallying

Red, Teagan, Isaiah, and Alejandro wasted no time running up to people passing by, their clipboards at the ready. I stood off to the side, my mouth clamped shut. A bunch of girls from my hip-hop class had shown up and begun a dance line near the sidewalk. They even had a radio set up, playing the instrumental version of Silentó's "Watch Me" song, but instead of calling out the real lyrics, they said, "Look, we stand with Liberty! Look, look, we stand with Liberty!" People couldn't help but stop and stare at them, and they made sure to hand each person a Dream Together card and point them in the direction of one of the kids with a petition. Now more than ever I wished I hadn't volunteered for petition duty.

I looked around. Isaiah was a few feet away and Alejandro and Teagan were on the opposite corner. No one was across the street. Perfect. I could have all the people on that side of the street to myself and, a small voice in my head whispered, *If you mess up no one will notice.*

I told Mama where I was headed and she insisted that Daddy cross the street with me. "Go get 'em, Gabby," he called to me as he jogged back to Mama and the rest of the chanters.

Mama had told me to stand where she could see me, so

Gabriela

I planted myself firmly on the corner. There were people coming from two directions. A man with two sons. *Don't bother him,* I told myself. *He's busy.* I said the same thing about the woman on her cell phone, and the couple holding hands. But I couldn't say the woman a few feet away was busy. She had her hands in her pockets and walked slowly toward me, as if she had no place important to be. I breathed in deep.

"Uh, excuse me?" I said as she passed.

The woman turned, already smiling. "Yes?"

"Hi." I waved. "Um, I . . . I'm out here, um I mmmean we're out here be-be-because Liberty Arts Center, is, i-i-it's dark. I mmmean, um, the lights went out—"

"I heard about that!"

I nodded, wishing she would just let me finish.

"Aaaand, we're out here t-t-today because—"

"Oooh, Gabby, good idea to come across the street!"

I looked behind me, and there was Teagan, hurrying over. I waited for her to keep jogging right on past me and take up the spot on the opposite corner, but she didn't. She stopped and stood right next to me.

"An-an-anyway," I went on, trying to pick up where I'd left off, trying to pin the necessary words down and push through my bumpy speech. But the only words in my head were *Teagan, what are you doing here?!* "Anyway, wwwwe're out here today b-b-because . . ." I stopped to take a deep breath.

"We're hoping to collect enough signatures to show the city that Liberty needs to be repaired as soon as possible," Teagan cut in. "Would you be interested in signing Gabby's petition? Gabby, wait she's going to—"

I was already walking away. Behind me, I heard Teagan say a rushed "Thank you!" to the woman, and then her sneakers were slapping the sidewalk as she ran to catch up with me.

"What was—"

I didn't let Teagan finish. "Why-why-why do you have to do that all the time? Jump in and talk for me? Y-Y-You act like you have to ssssave me, like I can't talk for myself. It's . . . it's . . . *annoying!*"

Teagan's face crumpled. "I didn't know—I mean, I wasn't—" This was the first time I could ever remember Teagan searching for words. "You didn't have to be so mean about it."

"I need to try this on my own, okay? I'm going to collect signatures on that corner." I pointed over Teagan's shoulder.

"I guess I'll collect them on the other end," she replied softly.

Gabriela

I went to my corner and Teagan went to hers. I turned quickly to see that she was watching me. When our eyes met, she turned away. *Probably waiting to jump in and rescue me again*, I thought. But I'd show Teagan—I could do this by myself. I stopped the next man who walked by.

"G-G-Good morning, sir. I wonder if you'd b-be . . . if you'd like to sign our petition."

The man looked confused. "Petition for what?"

My face grew hot. "For, um, L-L-Liberty Arts C-Center? It needs, well, i-i-it's in the d-dark and—" I stopped myself this time. "Liberty Arts Center had a power outage and it needs, um, repairs. We are out here today p-p-petitioning the city to, um, uh"—I groped around for the word— "p-prioritize Liberty's rrrrr-repairs. Will you sign?"

"Of course. I went to your Rhythm and Views show a few years back. It was something else."

After the man walked away, I looked down at his loopy signature on the first line of my petition. I'd done it all by myself without needing to be rescued. *See, Teagan—I can do it.*

After that it got a little bit easier each time. My stutter still tripped me up a bunch of times, but I pushed through and got my point across as best I could. By the time the rally was over, I'd gotten two full pages of signatures.

Daddy came back across the street to get Teagan and me and said, "Great job, kiddo!" when I showed him my petition pages. Teagan just gave a weak smile. We didn't say anything to each other as we crossed the street. She didn't say anything to me when we walked around the corner of the Liberty building and saw the finished mural, either.

The mural was gorgeous—colors on top of colors, melding together into three giant hearts. I don't know if Mr. Harmon meant it this way, but to me, the three hearts represented the dance and visual arts departments, and our little poetry group. The chaotic colors on top of one another made me think about how we were so on top of each other in the rec room, and I let out a little laugh. Like Red's poem, the community had taken something chaotic and made it into art.

But the mural wasn't the only thing on the wall. All around the mural, people had taped up big paper hearts and written on them. Each heart finished the sentence, "I love Liberty because . . ."

"What do you think?" Amelia asked, coming up beside me. "We were talking about what we loved about

Liberty while painting, and everyone's statements were so beautiful, I thought we should write them down."

"They're amazing," I said. I slowly walked down the wall, reading each heart.

Because Liberty is full of art and history! That was Ameila's handwriting.

Because the arts are what make us human! Mrs. Blake.

Because I get to dance tap and hip-hop at the same time! Sharday, one of the girls in the dance line.

Because I meet people here who are different than me. Delilah, one of Mama's senior dancers.

"Pretty neat, huh, cuz?" Red joined us by the mural. "I'll admit I abandoned my petitions post for a while to come see what was happening over here. Not that I didn't get an *awesome* amount of signatures." He handed me his petition sheets.

Alejandro gave me his, too, and then Isaiah said, "Here you go," and handed me two stacks of petitions. "Mine and Teagan's."

I glanced up to see Teagan staring at the mural a few feet away, a sad expression on her face. Had I really been that mean?

I pushed the thought away and clipped everyone's sheets to the top of my own clipboard. They all had more signatures than me, but that was okay.

Rallying

"Hey, guys!" Bria came running up. "We sold forty bracelets! Looks like we'll be making more!"

"I got one!" Amelia said, holding up her wrist. The blue matched the sky above, the same color as our ballet costumes for Rhythm and Views. My stomach did a little flip flop. Mama told me yesterday that we needed to hear from the city before any decisions were made. I was trying my best to believe the show would go on.

"Looks like they're starting to clean up," Amelia said. Mama was doing her director thing, telling everyone what needed doing.

"I can help with the paints," I said.

"And I'll help take down the info table," Teagan said. She booked it across the asphalt and toward the parking lot. A tiny part of me wanted to chase behind her, but what would I say if I did? I'd meant what I'd said earlier, even if it came out a little bratty.

Alejandro and Bria tackled one end of the mural cleanup. Red, Isaiah, and I tackled the other, beside a ladder with an open jar of paint on one of the steps. I placed the clipboard with the petitions on the ground beside me.

"Your mom said we needed at least two hundred signatures to convince the city to make Liberty a priority, right?" Red said as he plucked a dirty paintbrush off of the ground and tossed it in a plastic bag. "How many do you think we have?"

I crouched down and spread out the pages of the petition. Each page had twenty numbered lines. There were thirteen pages with all twenty lines full. My heart did a happy skip.

"More than enough!" I said, standing up. It took me a minute to do the math in my head. "We've got two hundred sixty if we only count the pages that are completely full of signatures. When we add in the signatures on the half-full pages, we'll have even more."

"We thought we couldn't do it—" Red began.

" 'How far that little candle throws his beams!' " Isaiah declared.

I was so happy, I couldn't even roll my eyes at Isaiah yelling out Shakespeare quotes that made no sense. I felt like I could jump. Soar. I prepped and did a double pirouette turn.

"You know, I can do that, too," Red told Isaiah.

This time, Red didn't have a garbage can to break his fall when he lost his balance. He fell into Isaiah instead, who said, "Many accidents are caused by imitation."

"Shakespeare?" Red asked.

"No," Isaiah replied, shoving Red off of him. "*Me.*"

Rallying

"Face it, Red," I teased. "You just don't have the skill."

This time I did a fouetté turn, thrusting my leg out as I spun.

"Gabby, watch out!" Red cried.

It was too late. I'd kicked the ladder. I spun back around just in time to see the can of dark blue paint fall off the fourth step. Right onto the signed petitions.

"Oh no," I whispered.

The next few seconds happened as if they were a movie. I watched them, but I wasn't really a part of them. Red and Isaiah dropped to their knees and frantically shook the pages of the petition, trying to shake the paint off. Teagan and Bria raced over to see what had happened, followed by Mama and Daddy. No one seemed to notice me standing there. I backed slowly away and then broke into a run until I reached the side of the community center, out of sight. Then I sat down in a patch of grass and dirt, the same words playing on a loop in my head.

This is all your fault.

Inspiration

Chapter 11

It wasn't long before I heard footsteps on the sidewalk. I looked up, expecting to see Mama looking down at me, or Red, or *maybe* Teagan. But it wasn't any of them. It was Amelia.

"Hey," she said. "Room for one more?"

My patch of grass was but only so big, but I moved over and pressed myself against the wall so Amelia could sit beside me. Amelia was always so perfect. I couldn't remember ever seeing her make a mistake. I made sure the knees of my old jeans didn't touch the knees of her clean, crisp white ones. I didn't want my ability to make a bad situation worse to rub off on her.

"I know that I ruined—"

She held up her hand for silence. "We finished the mural. It's beautiful—"

Inspiration

"Why did I think I could ever be in charge of anything in the first place?"

Amelia went on, as though I hadn't spoken. "And we got a lot of donations toward the Dream Together campaign. I'm hearing between eight hundred and a thousand dollars."

"I ruined everything." Tears pushed at the back of my eyes.

Amelia sighed. "You did not. No one is mad about the petition. We're just all excited about what we accomplished today."

"B-B-But—but it's not enough, is it?" I yanked a handful of grass from the earth and tossed it on the ground in front of me. "It's llllllike we're ta-ta-taking one step fffffforward and then taking two steps ba-ba-ba-back!"

"But we still took that one step, and that matters. It's like dancing, Gabby. You can't have a dance if you never take the first step. Like today. I saw you struggling to talk to those strangers, but you took one step and then another, and before you knew it, you were collecting signatures left and right."

"Yeah, and then I spilled p-paint all over them," I muttered, yanking up another handful of grass. "Sometimes it's not even worth it to work through my words. I sh-sh-should have just worked on the mural."

Gabriela

"Can I tell you something, Gabby?"

I shrugged. Amelia took that as a yes and went on. "The other night, when your mom and I were running rehearsal, you got up to share a poem with Red. I should have been watching the senior girls, but I was watching you. I saw that you were scared, but you recited the poem anyway. That's pretty big." She nodded, as if confirming something to herself. "You kind of inspired me that day."

My head snapped up. "What? Me inspire you?"

"Yeah," Amelia replied, laughing. "I struggle with my words, too. I'm dyslexic. When I read, it seems like the words on the page play tricks on me, changing directions, letters moving from one place to another. But I fight. Just like you."

I stared at Amelia, beautiful Amelia, who Mama said was flawless. Even now, after hours in the sun, helping people paint, Amelia's bun wasn't the slightest bit messy, her pink-tinted lip gloss unsmudged. I didn't even see any paint on her hands. I had always thought everything came easily to Amelia, but I guess I was wrong. Without really knowing it, I moved away from the wall, little by little, until my knee was touching hers. She didn't seem to mind.

"What are we going to do now?" I asked.

Amelia looked at me. I looked back at her. We shook our

heads. Then we sat there, Liberty looming over us, big as the question neither of us could answer.

The next day, Monday, I tried to clear my head and not think about all of the problems with Liberty. But the one thing I couldn't stop thinking about was Teagan. Even though I knew what I'd said to her at the rally had to be said, maybe she was right: I didn't have to be so mean about it. That night, I went to my room, climbed up on my bed, and FaceTimed her.

"Hi," she said when she picked up.

"H-H-Hi," I replied awkwardly. We hadn't spoken in more than twenty-four hours—a record for us.

"So," she said.

"So," I said.

There was a long, uncomfortable silence that felt two decades long.

"I'm . . . I'm sssssorry for snapping at you y-y-y-yester-day," I said, at the same time Teagan blurted out, "I'm sorry for jumping in and correcting you and finishing your sentences all the time." Teagan went on. "It's just that you're my best friend in the whole wide world and sometimes when I see you struggling with your words, I want to help."

"I get th-th-th-that," I said. "But I'm not . . . I'm not

struggling, even though it sssssseems like I am. I'm—I'm triumphing over it, like Mama says, or at least tr-tr-trying to. So when you cut me off and r-r-rescue me, you're not really giving me the ch-chance to do that."

"Oh." Teagan looked and sounded more miserable than she had before. "I've really been messing up, huh?"

"No," I said firmly. "You just didn't kn-know and you were tr-tr-trying to help. Maybe . . . maybe from now on, you can hhhelp me by just letting me finish what I'm saying, even if it ssseems like I'm str-str-struggling."

"I can do that," Teagan said, brightening a little.

I nodded. "Thanks."

There was another awkward silence, and then Teagan said, "Hey, Isaiah taught Red and me about a new type of poetry yesterday. Have you ever heard of limericks?"

"L-Limer-*whats*?"

Teagan giggled. "Okay, guess not. They're short, funny poems that follow the rhyme scheme A-A-B-B-A. Here's one he made up about Red: There once was a boy named Red. He fell down and bumped his head. He screamed, 'Oh, the pain! I might go insane! No, I'll just rub it instead.'"

I laughed. Then we spent the next hour on the phone, coming up with limericks. And when my words got caught, Teagan waited while I figured out how to set them free.

Until Further Notice

Chapter 12

A few days later, Mama finally heard from Ms. Santos. When Red and I asked her what she'd said, Mama would only reply, "Mr. Harmon and I are meeting at Mount Calvary. Let's go."

She piled us into the car, and we rushed over to the church. Teagan and Mr. Harmon arrived right after us.

"What's going on?" Mr. Harmon asked.

"Nothing good," Mama replied. Then she pulled out her cell phone, dialed a number, and put the phone on speaker. I didn't recognize the woman's voice on the other line until Mama said, "Julia, I'm here with Louis, like you asked."

"Thank you, Tina. Good morning, Louis."

"I'm hoping 'good morning' means you have good news to share?" Mr. Harmon said.

Gabriela

"I'm afraid not," Ms. Santos replied. Mama started doing her Pilates breaths. "And I'd like to apologize for the lack of communication—I didn't want to get your hopes up. I heard your rally was quite successful, though. I've always been impressed with your group there."

Get on with it, I thought. That part about our hopes was worrying me.

"Anyway," Ms. Santos continued, "the city did want to support Liberty and did a more thorough inspection of the building to estimate the labor costs. Unfortunately, it turns out there is a lot more than a faulty electrical system. In fact, and I'm so sorry to have to say this—"

"Will you hold off a minute, Julia?" Mama asked.

"Yes, of course."

"You three, go upstairs," Mama told us.

The tone of her voice suggested there was no point in arguing, and I could hardly blame her after how I'd ruined the petitions. But we still had to fix what we messed up, and I wasn't going to miss what Ms. Santos had to say about Liberty's future. So I led the way out of the rec room and into the hallway. But I stopped there, just beyond the doorway to the rec room where we could still hear without being seen.

"Okay, Julia. Go ahead," Mama said, at the same time a voice behind us said, "Good morrow!"

Until Further Notice

I jumped. Red and Teagan did, too. We turned around to find Isaiah strolling down the hallway toward us, wearing a T-shirt that read *I'm handsome* and *a poet*.

"Shhhhhhh," Teagan hissed.

"—sorry to have to deliver this news," Ms. Santos was saying, "but the repairs necessary are so extensive, the city is considering just closing down the building altogether."

The loud outburst from Mr. Harmon and Mama drowned out Teagan's gasp and Red shouting, "No!" I couldn't think of a single thing to say.

"The city rep will get back to me with the final decision, which I will relay to you immediately. However, in the meantime, I think you need to do whatever it takes to demonstrate to the city why the center is so essential to the community."

Suddenly, words came bursting out of me. "B-Because Mrs. Blake says the arts m-m-make us human!" I yelled, running back into the rec room.

Teagan, Red, and Isaiah were right behind me. Mama and Mr. Harmon did not seem at all surprised to see us.

"Yeah, and because after my grandma died, the only thing that seemed to make my grandpa happy was coming here to teach!" Teagan explained.

"And because I found friends here," Isaiah put in.

Gabriela

"Exactly," I yelled. "And b-b-because Liberty is a second home to people like Stan and . . . and me!"

"Yeah, and because . . . because . . ." Teagan paused, then exclaimed, "I got it!"

"Sounds like things are getting exciting there," I heard Ms. Santos say. "I'll be in touch—"

"Wait!" Mama said. "Julia—is there any chance all this will be wrapped up in the next couple of weeks?"

The show.

"I don't think so, Tina. I'm sorry. I'll be in touch." Ms. Santos hung up, leaving a stunned silence behind.

"W-Wait. Is Rhythm and V-V-Views going to be c-c-c-canceled?" I asked, my heart sinking.

"Let's talk about that later, Gabby," Mama said, resting her hand gently on my shoulder. "Teagan, what were you saying?"

"That we already have a million reasons—well, seventy-eight to be exact—why the community needs Liberty. All we need to do is show them to the city!"

The Because statements! Leave it to Teagan to count them. I imagined taking pictures of all of the statements written in the hearts, sticking them in a big envelope, and mailing it to Ms. Santos. It wasn't exactly as official as a petition, but it might work. The city would see how important

Liberty was to the community, invest in the repairs, and Rhythm and Views would take place, just like it always had. Just like it always should.

Teagan continued. "And what if we film people reading their Because statements on the mural and make the clips into a video to send the city?" That was an even better idea than pictures and a big envelope. Teagan was on a roll.

"I'll do better than that, my friend," Red said. "What if we already had video of people reading their Because statements?" He reached for his phone in his pocket.

"You don't!" Teagan said.

"Oh, but I do. Thought they might make good material for a poem someday, so I videoed a bunch of people reading their statements after they'd painted them."

There was a long silence before Mr. Harmon said, "You know, we really should just hand the center over to you three—you've got everything all figured out."

By the time we got back home, Daddy was home from work and sitting at the kitchen table. Mama let Red and me explain the plan to him, while she nodded her approval.

"So do you have time to help with the video?" I asked.

"Of course," Daddy replied, grinning.

Gabriela

As Red began telling Daddy more about the Because videos, the tap dancers started up in my belly again.

"Mama," I blurted out. "Is the ssssshow going to be can-can-canceled?"

Red and Daddy stopped talking at once. Mama sighed. "Not canceled, Gabby. Not yet, at least. Just postponed."

"Until when?" Red asked.

"Until further notice," Mama replied. "We'll continue rehearsing, of course, but at this point, we're just not sure when the show will be. Hopefully, before the end of the summer." Mama's voice didn't have all that much hope in it.

Until Further Notice
Three words that mean
Maybe
Possibly
Or sometimes, never ever
Until we raise enough money
To equal hugely expensive
Until we can make the city
Pay more attention
Until we can show the world
Why Liberty is important

Until Further Notice

Why it matters, why it's more than
Just a center, a building, a place
To create
Until further notice
Until we can prove
Until then
No Rhythm
No Views

Because

Chapter 13

I woke up the next morning with the word "until" still imprinted on my thoughts like a brand. It was up to us—the Liberty community—to prove that the center was important and we'd do it, starting with the Because video. I went downstairs and found Daddy sitting at the kitchen table with his laptop.

"Mornin', kiddo. I'm almost done with the video. Want to see?"

Already? We had briefly discussed the video last night, but I thought we were going to work on it together today. My face must have shown my disappointment.

"I know you wanted to help with the editing, kiddo," Daddy said, "but time is of the essence in these things."

I knew that. I did. We couldn't prove how important Liberty was without the video, but I'd still wanted to help. Somehow, the night before, I'd convinced myself that if I did, I'd make up for causing the blackout, destroying the petitions, ruining Rhythm and Views. Everything. I grabbed a bowl for cereal and slammed the cabinet shut a little louder than I'd meant to.

"I really am sorry, Gabby," Daddy said. He came over to the counter. "How about this. You didn't film a Because video. Why don't we do that and then we can edit that in together?"

I appreciated Daddy's offer, but that would require me to talk on video; I wasn't sure I was ready for that. But then again, this was for Liberty. For Rhythm and Views, for Mama and Stan and Mrs. Blake. For me.

"Okay," I said.

That same evening, Teagan joined us for dinner. Knowing how much she loved video editing, I convinced Daddy to let her add the credits at the end. She pulled out a flash drive, did the quickest edit I've ever seen, and suddenly we were on our way to Mount Calvary to show Mama and Mr. Harmon.

We were at the church and standing in the rec room in no time. Mama and Mr. Harmon had been spending a lot of time there lately, even when there weren't any classes, brainstorming and discussing every little thing. We found them doing just that. When we walked in, they looked up, clearly surprised to see us.

"Robert?" Mama said. "We weren't expecting all of you to come by."

"I know," Daddy said, sounding as excited as a kid himself. "But we've got something to show you all. Louis, do you mind?" He gestured at Mr. Harmon's folding table.

"Be my guest," Mr. Harmon replied, looking both confused and curious at the same time.

Daddy set up his laptop and prepared the video. Then he pulled the table away from the wall and closer to where Mama sat with Mr. Harmon. "Prepare to be blown away," he said, and hit PLAY.

There, on the screen, were all of the reasons everyone loved Liberty, one reason flowing right into the next.

"Because Liberty shows us that dance has history." Amelia.

"Because at Liberty my tutu was blue!" Taylor.

"*<p>Because all languages are welcome here!</p>*" Teagan.

"It's written in HTML," she explained.

Leave it to Teagan to write her sign in code.

Because

"Because dancing brings me joy!" A senior dancer.

"Because Liberty helps me forget how much I miss my mom." Red.

Teagan and I looked at Red. He looked away. "It's true," he muttered.

My face crumpled. So did Teagan's.

"Look, don't go feeling all bad for me and saying 'awwwww' or anything," Red said, and made a big show of shifting his attention back to the video.

"Because art class is my favorite hour of the week." Mrs. Blake.

And then mine. "Because Liberty is where I met my best friend."

Teagan blushed. I smiled at her from the other side of the table.

Silence followed the credits. Then a sniffle. And another. Mama was crying! Even Mr. Harmon was dabbing at his eyes.

"We need to post this right away," Mama said, wiping her eyes.

"On it," Teagan replied. "Mr. McBride, do you mind if I use your laptop for a minute?"

Daddy said he didn't mind one bit. Quick as a flash,

Gabriela

Teagan connected to the church Wi-Fi and posted the video to the Liberty Facebook page, making sure to tag Ms. Santos and the city council.

"Repost the link to the Dream Together page, too," I added.

Maybe, just maybe, if we kept our fingers crossed, the city would finally see how much the community *needed* Liberty.

And maybe, just maybe, the show would go on.

Where Everyone Can Hear

Chapter 14

ello? Julia?"

We were getting ready to leave for Mount Calvary just a few days later when Mama's phone rang. Red and I were on our way outside to wait for Mama in the driveway. We stopped in our tracks by the front door.

There wasn't much to hear—Mama was doing a whole lot of "uh-huh-ing" and "I see-ing." But suddenly she burst out with, "That's excellent news!"

Mama hung up with Ms. Santos and was on the phone with Mr. Harmon a moment later.

"Just heard from her, Louis. The council was *very* impressed with our video and other efforts on behalf of Liberty so far. They are setting their budget for next year on the thirty-first. The final materials estimate is twenty thousand—"

Gabriela

Red and I looked at each other. *Twenty thousand dollars?!*

"If we can raise twenty thousand with Dream Together by then," Mama went on, "The city can commit to covering all remaining costs. Can you believe it?"

I couldn't. We were closer than ever to getting Liberty back! Red and I bounded down the front steps. I leapt skyward, executing a full-split leap in the air.

"Should I try that one?" Red asked.

"Um, I'm thinking no," I replied, laughing.

"Wooo-hoooo!!" Mama said as she came outside to join us in the driveway. "Did you two hear that?"

"YES!" Red and I said at the same time.

"But how are we going to raise twenty thousand dollars?" I said, climbing into the car.

"And by 'we' Gabby means everyone, including me and her," Red said. "We really do want to help, Aunt Tina. We're part of the Liberty community, too." I gave Red a little nod. Well said.

Mama didn't answer right away. I got the sense that she was choosing her words very carefully. "You two and Teagan were a huge help at the rally and with the video. You just keep making those bracelets. Every little bit helps."

Where Everyone Can Hear

"But what else can we do?" I asked. I still didn't feel like I had made up for causing the outage in the first place, and I was getting tired of making bracelets. I wanted to help. *Really* help.

"I'll think about that," Mama said, "but right now, you need to just be patient and leave the rest to the grown-ups. Everything will work itself out in the end." Mama pulled out of the driveway and started up the street.

"B-B-B-B-But how do you kn-kn-know that?" I asked, as we came to a stop in front of the small park two blocks from our house.

"It just will," Mama said firmly. "No one is going to let Liberty disappear."

I crossed my arms over my chest as the sounds of drum-beats hit my ears—a guy playing the bongos at the edge of the park. My heart pounded like his hands hitting the drums. How were we ever going to make up for causing that outage? I looked at Red. He shrugged as if to say, "What else can we do?" Once we got to Mount Calvary, Red and I let Mama go inside.

"Are we just going to keep making friendship brace-lets?" I said.

"Nope, we are not," Red replied. "If we want to really

make a difference in this campaign, it's time to strategize. And I know four people who will be happy to help."

"What about one of those local commercials?" Bria said, after we'd explained needing to raise twenty thousand dollars in the next two weeks and everyone had picked their jaws up off the floor. We had called an emergency poetry session. "My neighbor did a commercial for his furniture store. It was a bit corny, but it got my mom to stop in to check out the sales."

"Where would we get the stuff to film it, though, and how would we get it on TV?" Alejandro said. "Bet we'd have to pay to get it on the air, and we're supposed to be making money, not spending it."

"True," Bria said.

Isaiah suggested an e-mail to "ask" for donations. Teagan pointed out that most people just deleted those.

"Wh-Wh-What about a wwwalk-a-thon?" I took a deep breath. My stutter was acting up more than usual. Mama's Tiny Tot tappers were getting on my nerves, too, with all their *tick-tock-BOOM* steps, as Mama called them.

Red said you had to get permits for stuff like walk-a-thons, which took a long time. We had only thirteen and a half days. It went on like that for what felt like an eternity, one person throwing out an idea and another shooting it down. This wasn't getting us anywhere.

"Okay," Red said sitting down in his chair, defeated. "I think we've done enough brainstorming for today. Let's move on to some poems."

Without thinking, I stood up. Anger and frustration— at the rec room, at the group for not coming up with ideas, at Mama for not letting us help out more—bubbled up inside me. I just wanted Liberty back. I wanted things to go back to how they were before.

"L-L-Liberty is more than just a center," I blurted out. Everyone's heads snapped toward me.

"It's us, it's me, it's the heart of all who enter
It's Mr. Harmon, Sssssstan, Amelia, and Mama
It's d-d-dance, it's theater, it's art, it's drama
Liberty is where my words can be free
It's us, it's you, i-i-it's everyone, it's mmme—"

I was competing with feet pounding, Mama shouting, and art students laughing, and for all I knew, they were laughing at me. But I wasn't done yet. I raised my voice above it all, words coming to me left and right.

Gabriela

"And now it's been d-d-dark
No light, no ssssspark
We're in this other place
My words, no l-l-longer safe
Are out in a world wh-where
E-E-Everyone can hear
Everyone c-c-c-can hear
Everyone can hear!"

A giant weight lifted off of me. All those words that had been storming around inside me were out now. The group applauded. Everyone, that is, but Isaiah. He sat perfectly still, deep in thought.

"That's it!" he whispered.

"What's it?" said Teagan.

"It's time to bring the center to the wider community," Isaiah said. "Where *everyone* can hear."

"Huh?" Alejandro looked from him to me and back again.

"So far, we've tried to bring the community to us, right, with the rally? But that was only a small portion of people—just those who happened to pass by Liberty. We need to get out there, where *everyone* can hear. Great poem, by the way, Gabby."

Where Everyone Can Hear

"Yes!" Teagan said. "Great poem. And I get it, Isaiah—'all the world's a stage'! We have to go out there and use it like one."

"Not quite the right reference, but I do believe I'm wearing off on you," Isaiah said. They started joking but I only half listened as I sat back down. That guy playing the drums had popped into my head.

"P-P-Performance in the park," I said. "We could get some dancers, do some spoken word. Take the whole park by surprise by doing a random p-p-per . . . show."

"Oooooo," Bria said. "Like all those videos when guys propose to their girlfriends by getting their friends and family to dance!"

"Yes!" I replied. We could perform and tell them about Liberty and hand out cards. "Teagan, if there are one hundred fifty people in the park when we perform, how much money do you think we could raise?"

Teagan scribbled in Cody furiously. "Maybe six thousand dollars, if the average donation is forty dollars?"

It wasn't twenty thousand, but it was something—more than a quarter of what we needed. Plus, whatever our friendship bracelets had contributed. That felt about right. That felt about equal to the damage I'd done by pushing that big silver button.

Gabriela

Mama's and Daddy's voices were right there in my head, though. *It's too big for just us kids to plan*, especially with "time being of the essence." I could hear their push back as if they were sitting right beside us. We couldn't afford to push back, not now. Teagan, Red, and I needed to fix the mess we'd made, once and for all.

"I think it should be a sssssurprise," I said. "All of the grown-ups are super stressed with everything else. Let's make this, like, a gift for them *and* the community. We'll surprise them by saving the day." It was true I didn't want to tell Mama because I didn't want her to stop us, but I could also picture the mask of worry sliding from her face and being replaced with a huge smile when we told her we'd managed to raise a ton of money.

"Yes!" Bria exclaimed. "I love surprises. Did I tell you guys about the time we surprised my grandma for her birthday and her pacemaker went off? She's fine, though, don't worry."

"Okay," Teagan cut in. "Glad your grandma is doing all right, Bria. The city is deciding on their budget on the thirty-first. The last possible day for us to do the park dance is Sunday the thirtieth. I think we should do it on Saturday, the twenty-ninth, just to be safe."

July 29. That was the day the show would have been. "Yes!" I said. "It'll be like our own little Rhythm and Views!" Everyone agreed.

Teagan-the-Problem-Solver suggested we do it in Lincoln, the big park a few blocks away from Liberty, then shifted in her seat. "Is everyone here going to dance?"

"Yes!" Bria cried. Alejandro and Isaiah looked nervously away.

"I'll do it if Red does," Alejandro said. "He was bustin' all those moves in poetry rehearsal and all."

"You are not ready for all the moves I *can't* bust," Red replied. "But I'm in. Anything for Liberty. Isaiah, what about you?"

" 'Our doubts are traitors. And make us lose the good we oft might win. By fearing to attempt,' " Isaiah declared. "It means—"

"It means yes," Teagan cut in. "I think we should post a video of the choreography of the dance we're doing so anyone who wants to can learn and join in. Gabby, will you come up with the dance and record it for everyone else?"

"Sure," I said, though I felt anything but. Choreograph a whole hip-hop dance? And for other people? I'd never done anything like that before. Whenever I wasn't feeling confident about dancing, I always went to Mama. Suddenly, I was beginning to regret not involving the grown-ups in this. But I wondered if maybe Amelia could—shoot! I jumped up, grabbed my dance bag, and bolted for the other end of the room, pulling my ballet shoes out as I ran.

"Fill me in later! I'm late for ballet!"

I thought maybe Amelia wouldn't notice, or that she wouldn't care that I was late, but as soon as rehearsal was over and I was pulling my street clothes over my dance clothes, she came over to me.

"Everything all right, Gabby? It's not like you to be late to rehearsal."

"Everything's fine, great. Actually, there's something I want to ask you."

"Go for it."

I told her all about the park performance idea. Amelia needed very little convincing. "I'm in," she said. "What can I do?"

There were a few minutes before Mama came to pick me up. We sat down and came up with a plan.

Cats and Choreography

Chapter 15

It turned out that not only was Amelia an awesome dancer, she was an awesome co-conspirator, too.

The first thing she did was somehow convince Mama and Daddy they needed a night to themselves. "A date night, Miss Tina," she said to Mama one day after rehearsal. "To get your mind off of all the stuff happening with Liberty. You won't even have to worry about Gabby and Red. I'll stay with them."

That's how, on Saturday night, Amelia ended up in my room, standing beside me, our reflections sweaty and breathless in the mirror above my dresser. My mirror at home wasn't anywhere near as good as the floor-to-ceiling mirrors in the dance studios at Liberty, but we'd still managed to choreograph a pretty good routine anyway, even with Amelia being such a bunhead. She might be able to do triple pirouettes on pointe, but I had mad hip-hop moves.

"It needs something more, though," Amelia said. She paused a moment to use the bottom of her T-shirt to wipe the sweat off of her face. It was the most un-Amelia-like thing I'd ever seen Amelia do. I stared. "What?" she said.

"Nothing." I used the bottom of my T-shirt to wipe my face, too.

Amelia smiled briefly, and then went right back to business "What are we missing?" she said, just as Red passed by in the hallway.

As if on cue, Red jumped into my room. "Me!" he said. "You're missing me *and* my signature step, the ever-classic running man." He attempted to demonstrate and kicked back too hard with his right leg. In an instant, he was on the floor flat on his stomach.

"If that's your signature move, I'm a little afraid," I said, laughing.

"Definitely the running man," Amelia said, still giggling. "But we'll have to teach that one to Red personally."

Amelia and I worked in the running man while Red went and got us some lemonade. "Thanks, cuz," I said, taking a big gulp. "Want to see the finished dance?"

Cats and Choreography

"Does your dad talk about computers constantly?" Red joked.

He did.

"Great," Amelia said. "Red can be our audience. Let's run through it once before we record it," Amelia instructed.

"It. Looks. *Awesome*," Red declared, when we were done.

Amelia held up her hand for a high five, the way she always did at the end of ballet rehearsal. "Ready to record the tutorial?"

"Um—"

"You are," Amelia said firmly. "You can do this."

I went down to the bathroom to change into the outfit Amelia had picked out for me: a pair of black leggings, and a lime-green tank top with a purple crop top over it. The crop top had the word *Dream* written across it, which I thought fit the moment because I couldn't believe what I was about to do: record a video of me teaching choreography. A video that who knows how many people would see. My mouth went dry just thinking about it.

"Okay, so all you have to do is stand right here," Amelia said, pointing to a spot a few feet away from the laptop. "Wait. Gabby, what's wrong?"

"I'm just worried that—well, my stutter . . ."

"Don't worry about that, Gabby," said Red.

"At all," added Amelia. "If it makes you feel better, here's what we'll do: Whenever you stutter a lot and want to stop and try again, touch your nose. We'll stop and re-record. How does that sound?"

"Perfect," I said.

"Great. Okay, the camera is here." She pointed. "Green light means it's on and you see how it says MOVIE RECORDING up here? That's how you know the camera is rolling. Make sure you look into it while you're talking. Okay?"

It was just like dance class. Amelia didn't give me a moment even to think before she said, "Action!" and hit the PLAY button. And just like that, I was face-to-face with, well, me. Just me. I couldn't even see Amelia or Red in the background. They had moved to the far corner of my room, out of sight. I thought about all the times I had taught myself new moves in my dresser mirror, talking myself through the instructions to each. *This is just like that, Gabby*, I told myself. *And it's okay if you stutter a little. Just say what you have to say.*

"W-W-W-Welcome, everyone, t-t-t-to my, um, the L-L-Liberty Park D-Dance tutorial," I said to the camera. "F-F-F-First, I will show you the ch-ch-choreography all the way through. Then, I will . . . will teach you how to, um, do each dance one step at a t-t-time. If you can't get one, d-d-don't worry. You know where to find me for some in-p-p-person help."

I took a deep breath. It wasn't perfect, but I'd gotten the words out. I'd said what I had to say, stutter and all. I looked over at Amelia and Red, who gave me double thumbs-up. *You can do this, Gabby,* I told myself, and launched into teaching the moves.

Sweat was dripping off my forehead by the time we got through filming the second verse of choreography. I only had to use our signal to back up and start over once when "slide" insisted on coming out as "sssssssssslide." But now that I thought about it, that might have actually helped get the essence of the step across. I took a swig of lemonade as Maya sauntered into the room and hopped up on Amelia's lap.

"That was great, Gabby!" She stroked Maya from her head to the tip of her tail. Maya let out a big purr. "You were clear, concise, and had a smile on the whole time to boot. I'm not sure I could have taught those steps better myself."

"I could have," Red said, with a smirk. "That was pretty great, cuz, but we all know my pirouettes are spinny-ier and my leaps are leap-ier than yours. Shall I demonstrate?"

Gabriela

"NO!" Amelia and I said at the same time. Maya let out a big *meow*.

"See, even the cat thinks that would be a bad idea," I said, laughing and shaking my head at Red. "But good to know you're willing should I ever need a clumsy, overly enthusiastic assistant."

"At your service, my lady," Red said, sounding an awful lot like Isaiah.

"Before we film the last bit," Amelia said, "maybe we should give people info about the rehearsal on Thursday?"

"Good plan." Amelia said we'd want a rehearsal to go through everything in person, which meant we had to get everyone participating to the same place without any of the grown-ups finding out. My palms had begun to sweat just thinking about it. But Amelia had said, "Leave it to me" and when I argued, she had answered, "Gabby, am I an awesome co-conspirator or not?" I had to admit she was. Amelia said she'd find a way to get the adults out of the rec room on Thursday night and offer to run the scheduled All Company dance rehearsal, which would really be a secret park dance practice.

I pressed RECORD and gave the necessary details for Thursday, making sure to mention that we have only one week to pull this off, so people had to practice on their own before rehearsal. Then all we had left to film was the final chorus.

This last bit of choreography was the part *everyone* would join in on. It was my favorite part of the whole thing, because anybody—from the senior girls to the Tiny Tots to Alejandro and Red and their two left feet—would be able to do these moves. I wanted Teagan and Isaiah and everybody to feel the same rush I did when I got to shout with my body instead of my words. There was nothing like it.

"Okay!" I said, turning to Red and Amelia. "Let's do this!"

People had eight counts to run to their spots, and then eight counts of punching their fists in the air. I got through teaching the next two phrases of movement with only one or two stutters and didn't even bother to signal Amelia to stop. Her nodding told me I was getting across what I needed to get across to teach these steps. Who cared if there were a few extra syllables in between?

"G-G-Get ready, dancers," I said, looking directly into the camera. "It's time for the big ending!" Amelia gave me another thumbs-up.

"This is the very last moment, so I want everyone to dance as big as they can with as much energy as they can." Beside me off camera, Red jumped to his feet, apparently ready to dance as big as he could with as much energy as he could.

"You're going to step forward with your right foot, then your left foot." I demonstrated, Red mimicking me just out of the frame. "Then you jump to cross your feet under you. After that, we'll spin to unwind our feet—" As I turned slowly around, I saw Amelia struggling to hold a very wiggly Maya. *Hang in there, kitty,* I thought. *We're almost done.* "W-W-We unwind our feet and then on the very last beat we're going to—"

Suddenly, I had an idea. I made eye contact with Red, which wasn't exactly easy because somehow his feet had gotten *more* crossed while he was unwinding.

"W-W-We unwind our feet and then we're going to strike a pose, which my assistant, Red, will now demonstrate."

"Yes!" Red said, jumping into the frame.

"No!" Amelia shouted half a second later. Maya dashed toward me in a furry blur. I stumbled and fell backward before Red had even hit his pose. Maya was on my chest and rubbing her face against mine in no time.

"Maya!" I groaned, picking her up. "Should we shoot that again, Amelia? Amelia?"

Amelia was doubled over in the furry chair, shaking

with laughter. Red had lost it, too, and soon I couldn't help but join in.

"Let's keep it," Amelia said. "Some people might come for the choreography, but stay for the cat."

"Are you sure?"

"Of course I am. Cats are like ketchup. They make everything better!"

Crisscross
My mind spins 'round
Feet fly forward one, two, three
Five, six, seven, here comes eight
I'm flying, flipping, floating free
Do you feel that?
Can you hear that?
Two dozen hands
Two dozen feet
Two dozen shoulders, knees, eyebrows, and toes
Silently shouting what my heart has always known

Five, Six, Seven, EIGHT!

Chapter 16

At the rec room that week, it was business as usual—except that I could hardly focus on dance or poetry because people kept coming over to me and whispering, "I've been practicing."

"That's great," Amelia said, after ballet rehearsal on Wednesday. "Sounds like we'll have a big crowd tomorrow!"

I looked to make sure Mama wasn't listening to our conversation. She wasn't—her face was buried in a copy of a book she'd ordered online titled *From Nothing to a Lot in No Time Flat: How to Hit Your Fund-Raising Goal in Less than a Week.* The grown-ups had been cold calling and e-mailing community members explaining our situation and asking for donations, and we had made what felt like seventy trillion bracelets to sell around town, but we were still about twelve thousand dollars away from our Dream Together goal.

Five, Six, Seven, EIGHT!

I had come downstairs on Thursday morning to find Mama snoring and drooling with her head down on the kitchen table. Daddy shushed me when I tried to ask if she was okay.

"Only seven hours' sleep in the last three days," he whispered. "Let her rest before she has to be at the church later."

I poured my bowl of cereal as quietly as I could, wondering if we should just come clean about the park dance. What if Mama loved the idea and had even more thoughts about how to make it successful? Maybe the park dance could push us over our goal if we had some help.

But then Daddy reached over my shoulder to pour milk on my cereal, like he used to do when I was little. If we spilled the beans about the park dance, and Daddy and Mama thought it was a good idea, they would pour on their help and drown us kids out just like Daddy drowned my cereal. It hurt me to see Mama so tired and stressed, but getting back into Liberty was my bowl of cereal and I would prove to Mama and Daddy that I could pour my own milk.

Now we just had to pull off a rehearsal without the grown-ups finding out.

Gabriela

"Tell Amelia thanks again for me," Mama said as she pulled into the church parking lot later that evening. Red had come along, too, under the guise of running the sound system while Amelia ran the "All Company rehearsal."

"I'm grateful to Amelia for stepping in tonight and for setting us up with this potential donor. We'll swing by on our way back from dinner to pick you two up."

I noticed that Mama was gripping the steering wheel so tight, her knuckles had turned a shade lighter than the rest of her hand.

"I'm sure this donor will get us what we need," I said, trying my best to look confident when Mama glanced at me in the rearview mirror. I didn't know who this donor was, but Amelia assured me he did actually have the potential to help our cause. I closed my eyes for a quick second, willing this mystery donor to hand over at least a few thousand bucks, then grabbed my dance bag.

"I have a good feeling about tonight," I said, getting out of the car behind Red. "You'll see, Mama."

Mama nodded. "Thanks, Gabby. Will you do me a favor? Will you dedicate your dance to Liberty tonight? Send some extra energy toward getting our home back? We need all the help we can get."

Five, Six, Seven, EIGHT!

"Oh, I will," I said. "You can be sure of that." I waved as she drove away, then followed Red into the rec room.

The scene in front of me reminded me of our first day at the church. People were chatting, excitement in their voices, ready to see what this was all about, ready to try something new. My heart started tap dancing. They were waiting to learn something new from *me*.

"Told you we'd come, Gabby!" Bria ran up to me, with Alejandro and Isaiah close behind. "You did great on the video, by the way. We can't wait to do the dance for real!"

"Thanks," I said. "Thanks for coming."

Besides the poetry kids, most of the dance company girls were there, plus Mr. Stan, and Mr. and Mrs. Blake, too. There were also two people I'd never seen before. A skinny woman with blonde hair streaked with hot pink and a tall man with dreadlocks.

Teagan and Amelia came up beside me. "Wait! I know him!" I said, pointing the to the dreadlocks guy. "He's the first person who signed my petition!"

He caught my eye and waved. I waved back. The rally seemed like forever ago. Back then, we didn't know if we'd ever be in Liberty again. We still didn't, but that was what tonight was all about.

Gabriela

As if on cue, Isaiah tapped me on the shoulder. "Just about time to start," he said, "and thus, I'd like to say, 'When you do dance, I wish you a wave o' th' sea, that you might ever do nothing but that.'"

"Uh, thanks," I said. Then I did a little curtsy to Isaiah. It just seemed right. Isaiah laughed and bowed back.

I turned to Amelia, who gestured to the front of the room where she or Mama usually stood.

"Over to you, Miss Gabby."

The taps in my chest picked up speed. I gave Amelia a small smile, then turned to face my students. *You can do this, Gabby. It'll be just like when you practiced with Maya this morning.*

Except everyone was a lot less furry than Maya. And a whole lot more human. I took a cue from Red's book and clapped loudly, giving my words a couple extra seconds to organize themselves.

"Thank you all sssssssso much for coming tonight. Is e-e-everybody ready to dance for Liberty?"

Forty voices shouted back at me, "Yeah!" Well, maybe thirty-nine. Alejandro was standing off in a corner, trying to look invisible. I was starting to think Bria had dragged him there. Still, he was there. I had to remember to tell him later how much that meant to me.

Five, Six, Seven, EIGHT!

"Sssso we're going to run through everything from the top, and then work in some spoken word that Rrrred and I have been trying out. We'll also figure out who can hand out Dream Together cards after the dance and all that jazz, and go over the plan for arriving at the park on Saturday. Sound good?"

Forty heads nodded.

"All right, then," I said loudly, as Amelia cued up the music. "Dance company girls, get ready on the sides; you come in on the faster music. E-E-Everyone else, stay to the sides and I'll cue you in when it's time. Brittney? You take center stage."

It had been my idea to start the dance with a soloist, and Amelia had suggested Brittney. I was nervous about asking her, but if she was still hung up on whatever upset her that day she gave me the dirty look, she didn't show it. "Absolutely," she'd said when I'd asked her.

People shifted to the edges of the room until it was just Brittney in the center. I nodded to Amelia and took a deep breath. *Here we go, Liberty. This is all for you.*

"Five. Six. Five, six, seven, EIGHT!"

When Mama picked us up that night, I think I may have floated into the car. Rehearsal had gone well, with the exception of Red hitting Alejandro in the back of the head during the whip and nae nae. But in the grand scheme of things, I was calling tonight a success. There was only one moment where I let my frustration over my words get the best of me, which Amelia took as an opportunity to suggest a water and bathroom break. A quick pep talk to myself in the bathroom stall and I was ready to get back out there. Liberty was calling.

"So what do you think, Maya?" I said, changing out of my sweaty dance clothes into my snuggly pj's and slippers. She was curled up in my chair, as usual. "Think this park performance will push us over our goal? We have only two days left."

Maya flicked her tail as if to say, "Why are you asking me?"

"Because, Maya," I said, climbing up to my bed. "Not getting back into Liberty would be like you never sleeping in my furry chair again. I'm sure you'd find another spot, but it would never be as good as this one. Am I right?"

Maya let out a little meow.

Amelia was right. Cats *did* make everything better.

Picnic in the Park

Chapter 17

*A*ll classes and rehearsals were canceled on Friday—we needed that time to raise money. We set the bracelets aside, and Mama and Daddy let us help with phone calls. We also had to confirm our plan for getting most of the performers to the park without the adults finding out.

Just when I thought Amelia couldn't possibly pull off another top-secret mission, she did. This time she asked Mama if the Senior Company could take the Junior Company out for a picnic in the park on Saturday.

This earned Amelia one of Mama's *Are-You-For-Real* looks when she FaceTimed Mama on Friday morning. "You mean to tell me the *seniors* want to hang out with the younger dancers? Are you sure about this?"

"Yes," Amelia said, nodding until she started to look like the bobble-head ornament in the rear window of Mr.

Harmon's car. "For a lot of them, this is their last year as center regulars. They'd like to spend a little quality time with the other dancers before they go. They love the juniors!"

Mama raised one eyebrow. Even I thought Amelia was laying it on a bit thick. Sure, the senior dancers were nice to us juniors, but more often than not, they treated us like their annoying little sisters.

"Why tomorrow?" Mama asked.

Amelia didn't miss a beat. "We realized last night that this is the only weekend everyone's free before the seniors go away. So it's now or never."

"And," I cut in, "tomorrow would have been Rhythm and Views. We wanted to do something special."

Mama's eyebrows went up, and she took a deep breath. "You're right, Gabby. Of course."

"So is it cool?" Amelia asked.

Mama sighed. "Yes. Someone ought to have some fun tomorrow."

"Great," Amelia said. "I'll swing by and pick up Gabby around eleven. Try to get some rest, Miss Tina."

"Yeah," Mama said, and then, "Oh, hey, Amelia—could you check in with your contact? He said last night he had to crunch some numbers, but we haven't heard back from him.

Picnic in the Park

I'm not sure what we're going to do if he doesn't come through."

"Will do, Miss Tina. Will do," Amelia said, then waved to me. "I'll spread the news about the picnic tomorrow, okay?" I gave her a thumbs-up.

Mama ended the call and put down her phone, only to pick it up to dial the number of another community member.

"Okay if I make some calls from the porch?" I asked Daddy. I wanted to text Teagan about the plan and was also afraid that if I watched Mama stress out any longer, I'd slip about the park dance.

Daddy nodded. "Sure. And thank you for all you've doing for the center these last couple of weeks, kiddo. I know you'd probably rather be hanging out with your friends."

"I'm happy to help, Daddy," I said. "Really."

Hopefully by this time tomorrow, that would be loud and clear. I just hoped our help was enough.

Liberty is more than just a center
It's us, it's me, it's the heart of all who enter

Gabriela

It's Mama's dream of arts for all
A place to catch you if you fall
The studios, theater, spots unknown
They live inside us
We are their home

I woke up Saturday morning with our performance song already on repeat in my head. My feet involuntarily started practicing steps while I brushed my teeth. As I passed Red's bedroom to head downstairs, I heard him talking on the phone.

That was odd. He usually talked to his mom later in the day. I hoped everything was okay. I'd made it to the bottom step when he flung his door open and came thundering down behind me.

"Who were you talking to?" I asked.

"Nunya." That was Red's way of saying "none of your business."

I rolled my eyes. Even Red being his annoying self wasn't going to bring me down.

Mama and Daddy were already at the kitchen table, talking softly. A brown bag folded over at the top sat on the table in front of them. They looked up when they saw Red and me.

Picnic in the Park

"I went over to Main Line Bagels," Daddy said. "Help yourselves."

I could tell he was trying to sound happier than he really was. Red and I sat down quietly. I pulled out a cinnamon raisin bagel for me and an everything bagel for Red.

"I just wish he'd let us know one way or the other," Mama said to Daddy. "I can't stand this limbo. And I'm not sure what more we can do between now and Monday morning."

"I know, Tina. I know." Daddy placed a hand on Mama's back and made gentle circles. Some of Mama's stress seemed to melt away. She gave Daddy a small smile, then turned to Red and me.

"Where are we at with Dream Together?" I asked, except it came out as "Woh wa ah wih ah fur fu?" due to the hunk of bagel in my mouth. Red translated.

"Still six thousand to go," Mama replied. She sat up straighter. "Hopefully, this donor will come through. It's a lot, but I don't mean to worry you two. I'm glad you're going to the park today, Gabby. What are you up to, Red?"

This was Red's chance to get to the park, too. "Actually, I was thinking I could go the park with the dancers and shoot some hoops while they make flower crowns or whatever else girls do at the park."

"Practice our leaps, probably," I said. "Get a group of dancers in a wide open space and we can't resist using it as a stage." I risked a wink at Red.

"Sounds like a good plan all around," Mama said. "I'm headed out to meet up with Mr. Harmon to discuss some things. I'll see you two later." She kissed each of us on the top of our heads and grabbed her keys from the counter. "And you, mister," she said, turning to Daddy. "You know your homework."

"Yep," Daddy said. "Make six thousand dollars appear like magic by the time you get back. And eat some nachos. I'm on it."

"What was that last part?" Mama asked.

"Nachos," Daddy said. "They help me concentrate."

"That's one hundred percent true, Uncle Rob. One hundred percent true."

Boys could be so weird sometimes.

Amelia picked us up at eleven o'clock on the dot. We said good-bye to Daddy and his nachos and then swung by Teagan's house.

"Hey, guys," Teagan said, climbing into the car with a backpack stuffed to the max. "I feel like I'm forgetting something. I've got two hundred Dream Together cards, four beanies to collect money in plus the one on my head, two bottles of sunscreen, some pens in case we need to write anything down, bug spray in case there are bugs, extra sunglasses in case anyone forgot some—"

"Whoa there, buddy," Red said. "I think somebody's a little nervous about today, huh?"

"Am not!" Teagan said, her face turning pink. "I just like to be really prepar—"

Red and I gave her twin looks; we weren't buying any of it.

"Yeah, okay," she admitted. "I've been up since five o'clock. I might be a tad nervous about dancing in front of a crowd. You all saw my running man. I have good reason."

That was true. Her running man looked like a limping llama at best, but I wasn't about to tell her that. I shifted to better face her. "It's not about the dancing. You know that, Teagan."

"Yeah," Red added from the front seat. "Who cares if your running man looks like a spastic goat careening down a treacherous hillside? You saw mine." Teagan furrowed her brow in either shock or disgust. Maybe both. I rolled my eyes at Red. Leave it to him to say what I was thinking. And more.

"What Red means is that nobody's going to notice if

you're doing the steps just right. It's about making a state-ment. Right, Amelia?"

"Totally. I can't wait to see you all knock it out of the park."

"You're going to do great," I said, finding Teagan's hand on the seat.

"Thanks," Teagan said. "I'd do anything for Liberty, but maybe next time we can save the world with HTML."

"Deal," I said, right as Amelia pulled into the parking lot of Lincoln Park.

The sun was out today and lots of families had packed for all-day cookouts. Anywhere there was shade, there were tables set up with dishes of beans or rice or ribs. And burgers—I *definitely* smelled burgers. My stomach growled.

We made our way to the area near the basketball courts, dodging little kids playing tag.

"You guys good here?" Amelia asked, once we'd found a spot near the courts and laid a blanket out. I nodded, though my insides were doing switch leaps, flipping and flopping on themselves. "Great. I'll go make sure we're all set up for sound."

"And I'm going to talk to the guys on the courts," Red said. "Give them a heads-up about what we're about to do. Only seems right if we plan to interrupt their game."

Picnic in the Park

"Sounds good," I said, pulling my phone from my dance bag. *11:34.* We'd told other participants to be in the park by eleven forty-five. We were to spread out, blending in with the normal park-goers. We didn't want to attract any attention before twelve o'clock, when Brittney would go out into the middle of the basketball court and start us off.

I sat down on the blanket next to Teagan, who was laying out the contents of her backpack in a neat row. Flyers, hats, sunglasses, sunscreen. I let my friend do her thing and lay down on my back, grabbing a corner of the blanket. At Liberty, I always rubbed the edge of the stage curtain to calm my nerves. The blanket would have to do for today.

As I watched the leaves sway overhead, I was reminded of a move in the dance and before I knew it, I was reviewing the steps in my head. The switch leaps in my stomach calmed down with each phrase.

I was just getting to the part where everyone joined in when someone shouted, "Go long!" A second later, a kid was diving for a football just inches from my head.

"Hey!" I said, propping myself up on my elbows. "Watch where you're—Oh. Hi, Alejandro."

"Hey there. Sorry 'bout that. Good catch, though, yeah?" He rolled over onto the blanket next to me.

Gabriela

"'Youth is full of sport, age's breath is short; Youth is nimble, age is lame,'" Isaiah said, running up to the blanket and giving a confused Alejandro a high five. Bria showed up shortly after. So much for spreading out across the park.

"What time is it?" Alejandro asked, just as Red returned from the court.

"Two minutes after the last time you asked," Bria said.

She had claimed a spot on the blanket, too, her head almost touching mine. Teagan's head was near my hip; Isaiah and Red were on her other side. The switch leaps started up again, but they were lighter this time.

"No really," Alejandro said. "What time is it?"

I pulled out my phone. "Eleven fifty-seven." Three minutes. I took a deep breath and gazed at the tips of buildings peeking over from the edges of the park. "We're big-time now," I said.

"Ready for crowds," Teagan continued.

"Skyscraper-high, touching clouds." All of our voices were one.

Here we go, Gabby, I said to myself. *Time to fly.*

Heartbeats

Chapter 18

Two minutes later, I was standing on the edge of a basketball court, all my senses on alert, as Amelia slowly faded in the music. This remix of "You Can't Stop the Beat," was slow at first, almost like the singer was whispering a secret. Brittney raised one arm above her head and then the other as the artist sung about unstoppable forces—an avalanche, the seasons, her dancing feet.

And Liberty, I silently added, as Brittney launched into a spiral turn. Contemporary wasn't my favorite style, but it was perfect for this part—the movements made what came next all the more exciting. As the artist sung about feeling lost and then finding her way, the leaps in my belly gave way to tap dancers pounding in my chest. We weren't about to let a little power outage stop the beating heart of Liberty.

Gabriela

Brittney finished out the slow part with a graceful a la seconde turn and then . . .

"FIVE, SIX, SEVEN, EIGHT!" I shouted right along with the singer and everyone else as the senior and junior girls rushed the court, then launched into the routine. A shot of adrenaline raced through my veins and I hit the steps hard. Had I kicked this high in rehearsal?

On the next verse, we turned to face the side of our "stage." The players on the other basketball court had stopped their game and were watching us. Kids were lining up on the play structure to get a better view, too. *Just you wait*, I thought. *This is nothing.*

The company members danced through the next verse and chorus, and if I do say so myself, we Liberty dancers rocked it. This felt totally different from performing onstage in a theater. We didn't have a captive audience politely watching whatever happened when the curtain opened. We had to use our movement to demand this audience's attention. I let go of the worries of the last few weeks and let the moves fly through me, my body shouting how much Liberty meant to me.

By the time we came to the bridge of the song, people had gotten up from their folding chairs and formed a size-able crowd around the court, cell phones held up to video us.

Heartbeats

For the instrumental interlude, the junior dancers backed away and let the seniors really show off. If anyone has ever said dancers aren't athletic, they haven't seen how these girls flip and leap across the pavement. I could only hope I would literally reach those heights when I got older.

The juniors joined back in for a chunk of unison, high-energy movement, and then it was just about time for the full group to join in. The voices dropped out and the music shifted key, building for a few measures while everyone else rushed onto the court.

With the start of the chorus, the singers came back in full force and forty bodies jumped in time along with them. Except—except there were definitely more than forty people on the court.

We spun around and behind me was the dad and two kids from the day of the rally, the ones I had decided not to bother with the petitions. They hadn't been at the church rehearsal but they were doing the steps. On my other side, there was a woman I recognized from Mr. Harmon's art class, and in front of me, a mom was dancing while holding one of the Tiny Tots. They must have found the video and learned the moves on their own. I actually got a little choked up—this community adored Liberty and was willing to do anything to keep us around.

Gabriela

And then I saw Teagan attempting the running man and couldn't help but laugh. All my friends putting themselves out there to keep the Liberty family together—I took all that unstoppable energy and funneled it into the last few lines of the song.

You can't stop the beat! We jumped and pumped our fists in the air.

You can't stop the beat! We spun in circles, the park whizzing by.

You can't stop the . . . We crouched down low, slowly rose up, and then I shouted the moves of our final step in my head while my body shouted them out loud: *right, left, cross-your-feet, spin-to-unwind, and . . .*

STOMP! We hit the pose in unison, more than one hundred hands in the air.

The audience burst into the loudest applause I'd ever heard. I closed my eyes for just a second, soaking it all in.

Now that we had their attention, Isaiah ran up to me with the microphone like we'd practiced.

"My name is G-G-Gabriela McBride and we are here today to t-talk about—no, I mean t-t-to celebrate—Liberty Arts Center." My speech was bumpy, but I went on. We had this crowd's attention. Now was our chance. "D-D-Did you like our dance?" I called out.

Heartbeats

The crowd erupted in whoops and hollers, the other dancers behind me joining in, too.

"Well, Liberty Arts Center taught most of us everything we know. It's an awesome place, and it means a l-l-lot to the community. B-But a month ago, the power went out and now Liberty is in danger of being shhhhut down forever if we can't raise mmmmoney for repairs. Is that fair?"

"No!" the crowd shouted.

"So will you help?"

"Yes!"

Suddenly, Red was beside me, reaching for the mic. It was his turn to shout the best way he knew how.

"At Liberty, we dance,
Paint,
Rhyme,
Dream
The door is open to all voices
To those who twirl, and those who write verses
You're free to be
Who you want to be
All we ask? Creativity
Liberty beats like a heart inside us all
Let's hold it up, now don't let it fall

Gabriela

I'm tellin' you
Liberty is worth the fight
Let's bring it out from darkness
back into the light."

The crowd burst into cheers and applause again. Some people even stomped their feet. The music started up again for a reprise of the final chorus as we'd planned. My heart pounded like a million tap shoes hitting the floor and in that moment, I wished Mama were there. You can't stop my beat, but Mama's beat is even stronger, and Liberty's is strong only because of Mama's passion for it. For us.

We approached the final line of the song again, but this time, some of us dancers positioned ourselves in the middle of the court. Right before the last note hit, everyone else crouched down and we did our most explosive move yet: full backflips together, landing just in time for the rest of the group to pop up and hit our final pose.

The crowd went crazy.

We held our pose for a few seconds, and then there was a second wave of cheering as we dancers jumped up and down and gave one another hugs.

I had paused for a moment to catch my breath when

someone picked me up from behind and spun me around. Amelia.

"That was amazing, Gabby!" she said, putting me down. "It was—I have no other words. Just amazing."

I beamed.

Teagan, Bria, and Isaiah didn't waste any time. They ran into the crowd and handed out Dream Together cards, and some other kids walked through the crowd with hats held out for donations.

Amelia and I started to make our way back to the blanket, saying thank you as park-goers congratulated us on the performance.

"Excuse me, miss?" Someone tapped me on the shoulder.

I turned around to see a man holding a microphone and another with a video camera perched on his shoulder.

"Cameron Fischer, CBS News," the man with the microphone said, holding out his hand for me to shake. "We received a tip this morning about your performance from a *very* enthusiastic young man."

So *that's* who Red was talking to on the phone this morning! I made eye contact with Red in the crowd and pointed to the camera guy. Red just shrugged and smiled, then started to make his way over.

Gabriela

"We were impressed with your performance," Cameron Fischer said. "Would you like to say a few words about Liberty's plight and why it compelled you to do what you did? This would be for tonight's evening news."

Me, Gabriela McBride, speaking on television. It would have been impossible a few weeks ago. I looked at Amelia. Maybe, just maybe, it wasn't impossible now.

"Go ahead," she said, giving me a big smile. "I'll be right here."

"O-Okay," I said to Cameron. "I . . . I . . . I can talk about Liberty." Over his shoulder, I saw Red and Teagan approaching us. "Can my f-f-friends be on camera, t-too? I couldn't have done it without them."

"Sure," Cameron said, then turned to the cameraman. "Tiger, are you ready?" Teagan and Red jumped in on either side of me, and Teagan and I shared a quick *Are-You-For-Real?!* look. She found my hand and squeezed. I squeezed back.

"And we're on," Cameron said. "Good evening. We are here tonight with the girls and boys of the local Liberty Arts Center." Cameron described the historic building and "Liberty's plight." He gave a brief recap of the flash mob, then held the mic out to me. "What would you like to tell our viewers about Liberty?"

"I—" So many words were zipping around inside me.

Heartbeats

How dancing at Liberty had allowed me to forget my bumpy speech and just be me. How hard Mama worked to make the arts accessible to the community. And how none of those words seemed to want to come out at this moment.

"I—" In the distance behind Tiger's camera, Isaiah was talking to an older gentleman. They were both laughing and gesturing wildly. Suddenly, I realized the old guy was Mr. Blake. Shakespeare, uniting generations.

"Gabby?" Teagan whispered.

I turned my attention back to Cameron. "I—We . . . we came here today because we wanted to show the community that Liberty is more than a beautiful historic building. Everyone—n-n-no matter who they are—can explore their creativity in our dance and art classes.

"But the r-r-really beautiful thing, the real work of art that Liberty creates, is the sense of community between our members. Kids fffinding mentors in older members. People having a safe space to be who they are and get support. We don't even really need a roof over our heads to make that happen—"

Red elbowed me.

"I . . . I mean, we'd definitely like to get back into the Liberty building." Cameron laughed. "The building houses our programs, which are great. B-B-But what I mean is . . ."

Gabriela

I looked over Cameron's shoulder at Amelia. "We need people's help to get back into the Liberty building because we want to welcome people into our community, our home, for many more years to come."

My heart was pounding so hard, I was sure the people watching the news would be able to hear it, but there were no more words whizzing around inside my head—I'd gotten all of them out.

"Liberty Arts Center, folks," Cameron said. "Sounds like a truly special place. If you'd like to help them out, visit the Dream Together link on your screen. You can also find the link on our website." Cameron waited for a nod from Tiger and then lowered his mic, officially ending the recording.

"Gabby, that was great!" Teagan said, while Red slapped me on the back.

"Truly great, cuz. Truly great."

Cameron told us what time to tune in later. We thanked him, and then it was just me, Red, Teagan, and Amelia, standing in the sun. If Liberty was a family, these were my brothers and sisters. We'd pulled off our plan to make things right at Liberty, and done it all on our own. Tonight, the whole city would see what we'd done on the news. Now it was time to tell Mama and Daddy.

Spirits Soaring

Chapter 19

"Mama! Daddy!" I raced into the house and found them at the kitchen table. Red was right behind me, another round of adrenaline pumping through our veins. We had checked the Dream Together page on the ride home and it was already up fifteen hundred dollars from this morning.

"Goodness, Gabby," Mama said, "you'd think the house was on fire the way you're running. How was the picnic?"

I grabbed a glass of water and chugged some down. "It wasn't a picnic."

"What?" Daddy and Mama said together.

"Hey, Aunt Tina," Red said. "When was the last time you checked the Dream Together numbers?"

"A couple hours ago. Why?"

"Maybe you should check them again," I said, hopping up and down.

"You two are acting like a couple of bugged PCs," Daddy said. "What do you mean it wasn't a picnic?"

"Will you just ch-ch-check the Dream Together page?" I asked. I pushed Mama's laptop over so it was within their reach.

"Okay, okay," Mama said. She clicked on the book-marked link. Daddy leaned in, and Red and I crowded over their shoulders.

One second ticked by, then two. The total was up about seventeen hundred dollars from this morning now. I held my breath as we waited for Mama and Daddy to react.

"I don't underst—" Mama started.

"I'm assuming this has something to do with your not-a-picnic?" Daddy said. "Spill."

I thought he'd never ask. Red and I told them how Amelia and I filmed the video tutorial on their "date night," and about the secret rehearsal on Thursday. We told them about the performance and finally about Cameron Fischer and the CBS News.

"Awesome, right?" Red said proudly, when we'd finished. He jutted out his chest.

"Actually, not so awesome." Mama closed her laptop and looked at Red and me. Red deflated. "I wish you hadn't kept this from us."

Spirits Soaring

"We wanted to surprise you," I said.

"And I understand that, but you all took on so much, even after I told the two of you multiple times to—" She shook her head again. "So much, it's unbelievable. I know you both love the center, but we could have helped you. You shouldn't have had to bear this much responsibility on your own."

"But why not?" I asked, with a little more attitude in my voice than I'd intended. "W-W-We messed things up at the center so we sh-sh-should be the ones to fix it. We've been trying to fix it all summer, but every time we'd shared an idea you all stepped in and only kind of let us help, and—"

"Hold up," Daddy said, raising a hand to stop me from talking. "You think you guys caused the outage?"

I tried to explain, but my words were being stubborn. This wasn't going at all how I'd planned. We were supposed to come home and Mama and Daddy would see the donations page and we'd hug and maybe get some ice cream.

Red took over. He told them how he'd turned on all the stage lights and how Teagan and I were trying to show our digital graphics when the power went out.

"And then I heard Ms. Santos talking in the hallway that first day," I said. "I heard her say 'fault.' It was us. I-I-It was our fault."

Gabriela

"So let me get this straight," said Daddy, looking at Mama and then back at us. "You think the two of you and Teagan overloaded the circuit breaker and caused the power to go out?"

Red and I nodded.

Daddy was quiet a moment, then shifted in his chair and looked straight into my eyes. "That may be what happened—it's likely, actually—but the center is old. Really old." He looked at Red, then back at me. "The wiring was a disaster waiting to happen. It was most definitely *not* your fault."

"But what about Ms. Santos?"

"I'm not sure," Mama said, "since I didn't hear it. But I'm guessing she was talking about there being a fault in the electrical system."

Oh.

Red had an expression on his face that said *What now?* There were a million words buzzing in my brain. I pulled out a chair and tried to pin them down. If the outage wasn't our fault, would we have been so determined to find a way to fix things?

Mama broke the silence. "I'm sorry you thought this was all your fault," she said. "I'm impressed you tried to take responsibility for your actions, though. That shows great maturity."

Red and I gave a small nod and said thanks. That's what we'd been *trying* to do all summer. Maybe we should have told Mama and Daddy we'd caused the outage. Maybe they'd have given us more responsibility from the get-go to make things right.

Daddy sighed. "We're sorry we doubted you when you expressed your ideas. And that we took over from time to time. It's frustrating to not get to act when you believe in something so strongly. That's what's been so scary about this whole thing for us—for Mama especially. If Liberty closes, then what?"

"But we're not going to close, are we?" I asked.

"With what you two and all your friends did today, hopefully not," Mama said. "No matter how much money the donations page gets, you did a lot of good today. We're proud of you. You should be proud of yourselves."

I was.

A few hours later, the four of us sat down in front of the TV, Mama and Daddy on the couch, me and Red on the floor.

Gabriela

We munched on a bowl of popcorn while the CBS News anchors did their opening segment and then the weather, until the anchor finally said, "And now for a story about a very special building in our city."

Some old photos of the Liberty Theater came on the screen as a voiceover gave a brief history of the building, including how Liberty Arts Center had been there for the last seventeen years. Finally, they cut to some footage of the performance.

"You choreographed that?" Mama said.

"With help from Amelia," I replied.

"And me," Red teased. "And Maya."

"We're here today with the girls and boys of the Liberty Arts Center," Cameron said. Goose bumps prickled my arms.

Daddy clicked the TV off after the Dream Together link appeared. I had seen myself on the news, but it was still a little hard to believe that I'd done an interview that thousands of people had seen. I twisted around. Mama's eyes were shiny.

"I don't know what to say, Gabby," she finally said. "I hardly recognize you these days. It's like you're a different person." She gave me the biggest smile I'd seen from her in weeks. "You've found your voice."

Spirits Soaring

I've found my voice. "I guess that's the sunshine to come out of these clouds, or whatever," I said.

"A saying worthy of Mr. Harmon," Daddy declared. He stood and pulled Red and me on the couch on either side of him. Mama joined us, sitting down beside me and opening her laptop to the Dream Together page again.

She rested her head on top of mine, and the four of us sat like that for a good long while, watching the Dream Together donations go up and up and up, our spirits soaring with them.

Victory

Chapter 20

Sunday morning, I woke up to Mama yelling for us all to come to the living room. I ran blurry-eyed down the stairs, Maya right behind me. Poor Maya. She thought I was on my way to crack open a can of cat food.

Mama was on her phone, saying, "Thank you so much," over and over again. When she hung up, she turned to us, her eyes wide with a combination of disbelief and sheer happiness. "Just got off the phone with Amelia's donor and . . . and—well, look!"

She gestured to her laptop on the coffee table. She had it open to the Dream Together page again.

I looked. Blinked. Had to rub my eyes and look again.

"We met our goal for materials!" Red said, his voice still raspy with sleep.

Victory

"We didn't just meet it," Daddy said. "We surpassed it by a few thousand dollars."

"And a few thousand more," Mama added, her voice shaking. "Amelia's donor is going to give me an additional check to go directly into future programs when we're back up and running."

The switch leapers were back in my stomach, only now they were leaping on a trampoline.

Mama clasped her hands and pressed them to her chest. She wouldn't take her eyes off of the Dream Together page, as though looking away would make all the donations disappear. "I can't believe it. I never thought we'd—"

Maya let out a loud, pointed meow from the spot she'd taken up on top of the coffee table.

"Something tells me she's not celebrating with us," Mama said, laughing.

"All right, Boss Lady," I said, skipping into the kitchen. "One dish of wet food, coming up." I supposed that if I were a cat, I wouldn't care about a fund-raising goal, either.

While Mama got on the phone with Ms. Santos, I ran upstairs and grabbed my phone. *Did you see the Dream Together page?* I texted Teagan. *Just woke up*, she wrote back. *Hang on.* Thirty seconds later, my phone was buzzing with dozens of happy face emojis.

Gabriela

Did you tell your grandpa?

Telling him now!

By the time I got back downstairs, Teagan had sent me a video of her and Mr. Harmon doing a happy dance.

Love it! I wrote back. *Talk to you later, k?*

Turns out Ms. Santos already knew about us reaching our goal and had already been on the phone with the city council herself, Mama informed us after she hung up. She was so excited she was bouncing on the balls of her feet.

"The city council is planning to hire contractors to get started on the repairs as early as next week. Should be done in about three weeks."

We stood for a moment in stunned silence. The only sound was Maya, loudly chowing down on her tender beef and chicken feast. Three weeks. Twenty-one days from now I'd get to go home.

"So Rhythm and Views is definitely on?" I asked.

"I would think so," Mama said. "I'll have to check on some things, but hopefully we can do it three Saturdays from now right after they're done with the repairs. How's that sound?"

Performing again in Liberty, with lights on, full power. It sounded like victory.

An Ode to Mount Calvary

Chapter 21

The next three weeks passed in a blur of rehearsals, poetry group meetings, and making sure we had all the details together for the big show. Even though the rec room was more packed than ever, for the first time in a long time, everyone seemed to be working together.

Sure, there were a few meltdowns, but no one grabbed her dance bag and stormed out or gave a Tiny Tot a dirty look. When Taylor went for Mrs. Blake's paint again, Mrs. Blake took her gently by the wrist and said, "I'll tell you what. One day, when you're not wearing your pretty tutu, I want you to meet me here with your mom, and you can mess in all the paint you want. But only if you stay with your group today and practice like Miss Tina wants you to. Deal?"

"Deal!" Taylor shrieked, and ran back to the Tiny Tots group where she belonged. The next day, Taylor arrived with her mom, both of them wearing sweats and smocks. Mrs. Blake made good on her promise.

That evening, as Taylor waltzed out, proudly holding a canvas dripping in paint, I went upstairs to the hallway, where Mama was reading something on her cell phone.

"Mama?"

She looked up.

"Do you think—do you think I could be in charge of the show's finale? I have an idea."

"Of course you can," Mama replied. Then she blinked hard, as if trying to bring me into sharper focus. "You're really like a new person, Gabby," she said softly, and for a moment I thought she was going to cry, before her face snapped back to serious mode. "It's going to be a lot of work, but after all you've done these past weeks, I know that you can handle it."

"All right, all right," Red said, clapping his hands. "I know we're all excited about the big show, but we've still got work to do, people. Work to do!"

It was Friday night, our community's last night in the rec room before officially being allowed back in the Liberty building tomorrow. After our final dance rehearsal yesterday, Mama and I packed up the ballet barre and a few other things from Liberty.

Mr. Harmon was packing up his art supplies tonight, but other than that, it was just us poetry kids there at the church. Our individual pieces for the show were all ready to go—we had practiced them at last week's meeting until we could recite not only our own, but everyone else's, too. Tonight was all about the finale.

"These are your writing prompts," I said, handing out strips of paper I'd printed out at home. "Let's write for ten minutes, and then when we're back in the circle, we can put the whole thing together."

I headed over to the yellow wall to write, even though I'd finished my own prompts earlier in the week. There was something I started this morning that I wanted to share before we left.

"These are perfect," I said, once we were back and everyone had shared what they wrote. "Ready to put it all together?"

"Yup," Alejandro said. "Let's make some magic."

Under my direction, we took lines from each of our poems and wove them together. We made suggestions for how to combine or improve one another's words, and most of the time we took the feedback without anyone getting mad. With ten minutes left in our meeting, we ran through

Gabriela

the whole thing start to finish, or as much of it as we could here in the rec room—the rest we'd figure out at the theater tomorrow with all the other people I'd enlisted to help.

"Hey, everyone," I said, clapping my hands. "Before we go, I . . . I . . . I want to shhhare one more th-th-thing." I wished my stutter would calm down, but I was figuring out that the bumpiness didn't just pop up when I was angry or frustrated. It popped up when I was feeling any strong emotion. I made a note to tell Mrs. Baxter about that new discovery. I called everyone back to the circle and opened my notebook to the page I'd marked earlier.

"S-S-So today's our last day here at the church, right?" Everyone nodded. "I was thinking we needed something to say good-bye to the rec room. Thank it for all it's done for us. We didn't get to do that before we left Liberty." Now that I was saying this aloud, it sounded kind of cheesy, but my friends didn't seem to mind. "S-S-So I wrote something. Maybe we can pass the notebook around and everyone reads a stanza?"

"You got it," Red said.

"Mysterious," Teagan said, giving me a *What-Are-You-Up-To?* look.

"Oh!" I blurted out. "And this poem is dedicated to Isaiah, for obvious reasons." I smiled at him across the circle.

"I'm honored, my lady," Isaiah said.

An Ode to Mount Calvary

I cleared my throat and read:

"We won't
Forget
That night for a long time
It tossed us upside down
Upset our summertime."

I passed the notebook to Red.

"No taps
No paint
No more recitation
And then a 'Good morrow'
Changed our situation."

Everyone laughed at that, especially Isaiah. Bria was next.

"Slick walls
Tight space
Floors gray like hard concrete
A wall of yellow sun
More noise than a swap meet."

Gabriela

She pushed the notebook to Isaiah.

"We danced
We spoke
Made art of many hues
You granted us the courage
To get us through our blues."

Alejandro took his turn.

"And so
Tonight
Parting gives us sorrow
And still we leave with strength
Ready for tomorrow."

Teagan pulled the notebook in front of her.

"For that
We give
You thanks from all our hearts
Your generosity
Will live on in our arts."

An Ode to Mount Calvary

Teagan smiled as she gave me the notebook for the final stanza.

> "Once more
> Good night
> Sun wall and concrete floors
> We won't ever forget
> Your welcome open doors."

It was silent for a moment, and then enthusiastic applause broke out on the far side of the room, startling us out of the moment. "Bravo, Gabby!" Mr. Harmon said, his voice all crackly. "All of you—bravo!"

"Are you crying again, Grandpa?" Teagan asked.

"What? N-No—got some dust in my eye from all this cleaning up."

"It's okay if you are, Mr. Harmon," Isaiah said. " 'How much better is it to weep at joy than to joy at weeping!' "

All five of us looked at Isaiah, eyebrows raised.

"What?!" he said. *"Much Ado About Nothing,* act 1, scene 1. Translation: Happy tears are better than sad tears." He sighed. "You guys are *really* going to need to start reading Shakespeare."

With less than twenty-four hours until we were back in Liberty, I could have cried happy tears myself.

Lights On, Full Power

Chapter 22

*B*zzzzzzzzzzzzzzzzz. *Bzzzzzzzzzzzzzzzzz.* I grabbed my phone off my nightstand and squinted at it in the early morning sun. Teagan had sent a photo of a cat in a party hat and a text that said *HAPPY LIBERTY DAY!!!!!*

"HAPPY LIBERTY DAY!!!" I shouted out loud to myself, throwing off my covers and scaring the living daylights out of Maya. She jumped from the top of my loft bed all the way down the floor.

"Ooops. Sorry, Kitty. But I'm pretty excited, aren't you?" I peered over the edge of the bed. Maya just flicked her tail. "Would you be more excited if I got you a party hat? No?" I climbed down the ladder. "Oh, well. Your loss."

After I texted Teagan a bunch of smiley faces, party hat emojis, and jazz hands, I brushed my teeth and took the fastest shower of my life. We didn't have to be at the theater for dress rehearsal until 10:00 a.m., but I felt like someone had videoed me on the time-lapse setting.

Back in my room, I double-checked that I had all my dance shoes, costume pieces, makeup, and some energy bars, then headed downstairs.

"Good morrow, cuz," Red called out from the kitchen table, as I dumped my dance bag on the floor. I hung my garment bag on the back of the pantry door.

"You mean GREAT morrow," I replied, grabbing some cereal from the pantry. "Seen my mom yet this morning?"

"Already at the theater," Red replied. "I think Uncle Rob is in the shower."

Of course Mama was already at the theater. I'm sure there were a million things to do for tonight, especially since we'd normally have dress rehearsal the night before the show. The contractors needed every minute they could get to finish out the repairs, so we were packing everything into one day—dress rehearsal at ten, rehearsal for the finale at three, show at seven.

I was just about to pour my cereal when Daddy came down the stairs.

"Good morning, kiddos," Daddy said, and then, "Freeze right there!"

Red and I both froze.

Gabriela

"Step away from the cereal," Daddy said to me. "I repeat, back away from the cereal."

Um. Okay.

"Today is much too special for boring old milk and whole grains. I was thinking the Waffle House. Any objections?"

"NO!" Red and I both shouted. We were in the car in less than five minutes.

One waffle with strawberries and whipped cream and two glasses of orange juice later, we turned into the Liberty parking lot for the first time since the rally. The switch leapers were back and using my breakfast as their dance floor. Cereal might have been a better idea.

Daddy pulled into a parking space, and I jumped out of the car before he had even pulled the emergency brake.

"Don't wait for me or anything!" Red shouted as I bolted toward Liberty's front doors. I flung them open and stepped inside the lobby.

The scent was the first thing I noticed. Like opening up an old book you've read a million times. I closed my eyes and took in a deep breath. And then another.

"Have the walls always been that color?" Red asked, coming up beside me.

Lights On, Full Power

I opened my eyes to see what Red was talking about. The city had repainted the walls. No more of Mama's apple green. "Nope, but I think I like them." The deep red color felt warm, like the den at Teagan's house where we watched movies during sleepovers.

The flooring in the lobby was brand-new, too. Black-and-white linoleum, glistening like piano keys. Red immediately started scuffing his feet across it.

"I see you doing that, Clifford Knight." Mama came striding across the lobby.

"Just breaking it in, Aunt Tina," Red said, but stopped anyway.

"It's so pretty!" I said, giving Mama a big hug. "Do you like it?"

"I love it," Mama said.

"Can we explore?" I asked. I wanted to find every little thing that was the same and all the things that were different.

Mama checked her watch. "Later. Dress rehearsal starts in five. I put the boys in dressing room four. Will you show Red where that is?"

"Lead the way, cuz," Red said. So I did.

Gabriela

Dress rehearsal was a blur of costume changes and lighting adjustments. Mama and Amelia ran the theater while Mr. Harmon set up the art show in the theater lobby. I took a quick peek out there while the Tiny Tots were practicing.

Mr. Harmon had displayed what he called his *Light Up Liberty Center,* a painting of Liberty with real tiny lights glowing in every window. It was the first thing you saw when you walked into the lobby, and students' artwork was spread throughout the rest of the space. People could view the artwork before the show and purchase pieces they liked during intermission. All money from sales went to scholarships for families who couldn't afford tuition for classes or the dance company.

"We're expecting a much larger crowd than usual," Mr. Harmon said, when I went over to congratulate him. "We had to prepare many more pieces. But I think it came together nicely."

"Exactly how many extra people?" Teagan asked, hanging up a painting of a marshy landscape. She was helping her grandpa until it was time to rehearse for poetry group.

"Well, the theater holds about four hundred eighty—"

"Four hundred seventy-six," I corrected. "Four of the seats don't work."

"They do now. The city fixed everything," said Mr.

Lights On, Full Power

Harmon, grinning. "And we're selling standing room–only tickets, so I'd say you'll be performing in front of five hundred people or so?"

Teagan's face turned the exact color of the murky water in the painting. I grabbed her hand.

"You're ready for this, Teagan," I said. "You know your spoken pieces inside and out."

"I know," she said. "But I've never performed onstage before. You've done this a million times."

"Just pretend the angels are sticking out their tongues," I said.

"Huh?"

I led her over to a bench so we could sit. "You know those angels that are carved into the front of the balcony?" She nodded. "One day when I was in the theater, I swear one of them stuck their tongue out at me. It was just a trick of the light, but ever since then, if I'm onstage and get nervous, I just imagine them making funny faces."

Teagan didn't look convinced.

"Like this," I said. I stuck out my tongue and crossed my eyes.

"Okay," Tegean said, laughing. "I guess I can try that."

The rest of the dress rehearsal sped by. Dancing on the Liberty stage again felt like stepping into my favorite pair of slippers after Maya's been lying on them. Amelia said I was smiling so big she thought my face might break.

With all the new stage equipment, the dress rehearsal ran over and I had only forty-five minutes to set the finale before we took a quick dinner break and got dressed for the show. A day had never gone by so fast.

I checked the clock in the dressing room. Five minutes to showtime.

"Places, girls, places!" Amelia clapped twice at the doorway of the junior girls' dressing room. I straightened out my sequin top for the opening dance number. "You ready, Gabby?"

"Seriously?" I raised my eyebrows at her.

"Never mind," she said, smiling. "Silly question. Break a leg out there, okay?"

"Yep," I said, and ran to find my place in the wings. Just a few minutes later, Mama kissed me on the head as she went out in front of the curtain to give her opening remarks. My hand automatically found the edge of the curtain and began rubbing it for good luck, the way I always did before I stepped out onstage.

"Good evening," Mama said. "Thank you for coming to Liberty's sixteenth annual Rhythm and Views show. It's great to see so many familiar faces here, but tonight I'd like to extend a special welcome to those of you who are joining us for the first time. As my daughter, Gabriela, says, we hope we get to welcome you into our Liberty home for many more years to come."

Had Mama just quoted *me*?

"Go, girls," Amelia whispered, motioning for us to take our places onstage. A million butterflies took flight inside me as I found my spot in the darkness.

"And now . . ." Mama said. "On with the show!"

Ninety minutes and six costumes later, the second-to-last number was onstage and we were waiting in the wings to do the finale. The rest of the show had gone really well. I'd only stuttered a couple times on my spoken word piece. Teagan hadn't barfed from nerves. And my dancing—Mama said it was flawless.

The music to the last dance number faded out as I rubbed the curtain for good luck one more time. Once the lights had faded to black, Teagan, Isaiah, Bria, Red, Alejandro, and I took our places scattered across the stage, me down-stage center. This was it. Of all the performances I'd ever done in my life, I had a feeling this one mattered the most.

The stage lights faded up, and I began to speak.

One Stage, Many Voices

Chapter 23

"L-L-Liberty is more than just a center
It's us, it's me, it's the heart of all who enter
It's Mr. Harmon, Mr. Stan, Amelia, and Mama
It's dance, it's theater, it's art, it's drama
Liberty is where my words can be free."

The rest of the poetry kids joined me.

"It's us, it's you, it's everyone, it's me."

Behind me, Daddy and Teagan's video began, and faces
filled the screen—snapshots of Liberty regulars throughout the years. They layered on top of one another, a collage
of the many characters that made up the story of Liberty. I
went on:

One Stage, Many Voices

"Liberty has people like no other
Like Mr. Harmon,
Who can name any color
And Stan, who, no matter what,
Always smiles
And Alejandro,
Whose laugh is so loud,
You can hear it for miles and miles."

Behind us, the faces on the screen disappeared and some music began to softly play. New photos came on—candid shots from rehearsals and art classes in the Liberty building. Teagan had added some original animation, too. A silhouette gracefully danced across the screen, and paint splatters began to appear around the edges. I resisted the temptation to turn around and look at it myself. For these next verses, Alejandro, Teagan, and Isaiah each spoke a phrase between my lines:

"Metal triangles tap on the floor."
"STOMP-shuffle-STOMP-shuffle-tip-tip-tap."
"While paint hits canvas."
"Swisssh. Dab. Blot. Repeat."
"And ballerinas warm up at the barre."

Gabriela

"Plié-two-three-four, and port de bras, ladies! Port de bras!"

Some of the parents in the audience laughed on that one. Bria's impersonation of Amelia was pretty dead on.

The music picked up in volume a little bit as the video transitioned again. Images from this summer began flying across the screen—the rally and mural painting, rehearsals in the rec room, a few snapshots from the park performance. The tap dancers filed in between us and began to tap softly on the floor, the sound of their taps punctuating our words. Red started these lines off, and one of us joined in on each couplet until we were all speaking together.

"We lost our building
But not our spirit
We live for this place
And let the city hear it"

(There were some whoops and hollers from the audience after that one.)

"We shouted, we painted
We danced, we screamed

One Stage, Many Voices

Our community rallied
We fought, we dreamed
We did what was needed
There was never a choice
We used our bonds
We raised our voice
We did all this
Without giving pause
We did all this
And more because . . ."

This was my favorite part. The lights had slowly faded during the previous lines and in the darkness, a few more people snuck onstage. Then a spotlight found one of the senior dancers and the video clip of her Because statement came on the screen. As her words were said on the video, she lifted her arms up and spun in a quick circle, a big smile on her face.

"Because dancing brings me joy."

Then the spotlight landed on Bria. She spoke out loud right along with her video.

"Because poetry group makes my heart sing."

Now the light found Mrs. Blake. She simply turned and looked up at the video where some of her artwork swirled onto the screen over the audio of her statement.

Gabriela

"Because art class is my favorite hour of the week."

And it continued like that, each person in turn "speaking" their statements, through taps, through pirouettes, through words, through art.

I had recorded one more Because statement and stood in the dark, waiting for my turn. The tappers had stopped onstage but not in my chest. Red, Isaiah, two kids from tap, Alejandro, three more dancers, and then me. I hoped I would get through my line without stuttering, but steadied myself in case I didn't.

When I felt the spotlight's heat on my face, I took a step forward and looked straight out at the sea of people in front of me.

"Because Liberty is where I found my voice."

And that was the cue—the stage lights came back up and everyone onstage began to speak at intervals, our voices overlapping like the colors in a kaleidoscope. As we talked, we made our way into one line across the front of the stage.

"Liberty is a place I call home."

"It's full of family. I never feel alone."

"The door's always open."

"It's a place I can grow in."

"Thank you, Liberty, for being patient with me," Bria said.

"For listening," Alejandro called out.

One Stage, Many Voices

"For helping me get out of my comfort zone," said a senior dancer.

"For challenging me."

"For saying my art, and me, are beautiful."

"For not giving up on us."

"Thank you, Liberty, for being our network and our strength," I said loudly, as the image behind us turned to one of hands linked together, superimposed over Mr. Harmon's mural. We moved closer together, now a large clump of people in the middle of the stage. Everyone said the final lines in unison.

"Liberty is more than just a center
It's us, it's me, it's the heart of all who enter
It's where our art and selves are free
So from the bottom of our hearts
THANK YOU, LIBERTY!"

And as we hit the last syllable, "You Can't Stop the Beat" burst through the sound system. We broke into the final chorus of the flash mob dance, more people rushing from backstage to join in. In front of us, the audience jumped to their feet. Halfway through the chorus, I realized I was singing out loud. I sang louder.

Gabriela

As the last line of the song approached, my heart gave a little squeeze. I had never felt so alive, but this would be over in a moment. I soaked it up for all it was worth.

Right, left, cross-your-feet. Spin-to-unwind, and . . . STOMP!

There was a muffled *poof,* followed by a huge cloud of thick, white fog. We had to move fast. The image behind us faded into one of Liberty, lights on, in all its glory.

By the time the fog cleared, the entire Liberty community stood onstage. Row after row of people standing together, arms linked.

"Thank you, Liberty!" we shouted.

You could've heard us—and the audience's standing ovation—from miles and miles away.

Giving Thanks

Chapter 24

A few weeks after Rhythm and Views, Liberty reopened and classes started up again.

I stood in the lobby of the building with Red and Teagan before our first poetry meeting since we'd returned. "Being back feels kind of like—"

I groped around for the word and when I couldn't grasp it, I looked to Teagan and Red. Neither of them could put the feeling in words, either.

Mama had asked the three of us to arrive for our meeting twenty minutes early to help her set up something else in one of the studios. She came out of the center office with a strange look on her face. The first official day back did feel kind of weird.

"Let's go, kiddos," Mama said, and led us down the

Gabriela

hallway. I hadn't been down this wing of studios yet since Liberty reopened. The fancy molding along the ceiling and doorways had been repainted a bright white, like clouds against the sunset of the red wall. I ran my fingers over the wood as we stepped inside studio five.

"SURPRISE!"

Studio five was full to bursting with people. Mama, Daddy, Mr. Harmon. Amelia was there, and Stan, too, as well as Ms. Santos. Bria, Isaiah, and Alejandro waved from one corner. Balloons were everywhere and there was a table laid out with snacks, drinks, and, best of all, brick-oven pizza from Antonio's.

"We wanted to throw a party in your honor to thank you three for all that you've done for Liberty," Mama explained, throwing her arms around Red, Teagan, and me. "So, I'll start. Teagan, thank you for all your help with the video at the show. That really touched me."

"Thank you for letting me dance in the park performance, Gabby," Stan chimed in. "I've never done anything like that before."

"Red, thanks for videotaping the Because statements at the rally," Mr. Harmon said.

And on it went, each person in the room thanking the three of us for something, until at last Mama spoke again, this time directly to me. "Gabby, thank you for being not just an amazing poet and a performer, but for being a leader, too. We are so proud of you."

The happy tears that had been building up inside since the day of the park performance finally came out. I gave Mama a big hug, and Daddy one, too. He handed me a tissue.

"Okay, let's eat," Mama said quickly. "Mr. Harmon, will you get the plates?"

As Red, Teagan, and I sat down to eat at the center of a long table, Mama joined us. "You know," she said, pulling two pieces of pizza apart. "I hope all this isn't going to your heads."

"Not at all," Red replied. "I'm not gonna start charging for autographs. Yet."

We laughed, Mama the loudest. "Provided you all can maintain your modesty, I'd like to tell you that you and the rest of your poetry group are kind of famous."

"Really? How?" Teagan asked around a mouthful of pizza. Bria, Alejandro, and Isaiah perked up, too.

"I've gotten some requests for 'those poetry kids' to perform at some other events in the city. I told them you all aren't really doing tours just yet, but maybe it's time to form an official spoken word group. What do you think?"

Gabriela

Red jumped up, almost knocking over his cup of fruit punch. "I think I'm in!"

"Me, too!" said Teagan. Alejandro and Bria nodded yes. Isaiah said, "Me three. Or Five. Whatever."

"But we start middle school next year," I said. I was more nervous about that than I wanted to admit. This summer had been so amazing; I didn't want it to end. "And I'll have Junior Company rehearsals. And then extra poetry meetings, too?"

"It will be a load, that's for sure," Mama agreed. "But think about it, Gabby. Without the poetry group, you never would have found your voice."

"And maybe it's time to take that voice out into the world," Red said. "Where everyone can hear."

Maybe it was.

 About the Author

Teresa E. Harris earned her bachelor's degree in English from Columbia University and an MFA in Writing for Children from Vermont College, where she won numerous awards, including the Flying Pig Grade-A, Number-One Ham Humor Award. She is the author of the picture book *Summer Jackson: Grown Up* and the middle grade novel *The Perfect Place*, which was selected as one of Bank Street's Best Children's Books of the Year in 2015. Teresa is a high school English teacher in New Jersey, where she lives with three very bossy cats. She spends most of her time grading papers, writing novels, and wishing she could dance like Gabby.

Special Thanks

With gratitude to **Leana Barbosa**, M.S. CCC-SLP, for contributing her knowledge of speech therapies and language pathology; to **Fatima Goss Graves**, Senior Vice President for Program, National Women's Law Center, for her insights into the experiences and perspectives of modern African American children; and **Sofia Snow**, program director at Urban Word NYC, for guiding Gabriela's poetic journey.

American Girl would also like to give a special shout out to **Urban Word NYC First Draft Open Mic** for inspiring the "First draft!" tradition for Gabriela's poetry group in this book.

Request a FREE catalog at
americangirl.com/catalog

Sign up at **americangirl.com/email**
to receive the latest news and exclusive offers

READY FOR ANOTHER
CURTAIN CALL?

Visit
americangirl.com
to learn more about Gabby's world!